HONOR AT LAST

AURORA HARDY

Epicenter Press

KENMORE, WA

⋀⋀⋀⋀ Epicenter Press

6524 NE 181st St., Suite 2, Kenmore, WA 98028

Epicenter Press is a regional press publishing nonfiction books about the arts, history, environment, and diverse cultures and lifestyles of Alaska and the Pacific Northwest. For more information, visit www.EpicenterPress.com

Honor at Last

Cover design: Scott Book
Interior design: Melissa Vail Coffman

Library of Congress Control Number: 2025945198

ISBN: 978-1-68492-296-3 (Trade Paperback)
ISBN: 978-1-68492-297-0 (Ebook)

To my son, P, daughter, R, and grandchildren
with all my love.
In honor of my parents.

Dear Reader,

The names of the villages in this story are written as those names that were used by people in the 1940s at the time of the story's beginning. In the modern day, Fortuna Ledge is now named Marshall and Tuckchuck is Takshak. The older terms were used as part of establishing the setting during the 1940s. Names of the main characters are in the Yupik language naming the person's position in life as 'father, mother, sister, brother, wife'. This use of the generalization of the names is because I do not have the original Yupik name and want to respect the person's identity by not giving their English name. This work is based on a true story.

Aurora Hardy
2025

THE STAGE
1930

IN 1800, JOHANN FICHTE WROTE IN his book *Vocation of Man* that "you could not remove a single grain of sand from its place without thereby . . . changing something throughout all parts of the immeasurable whole." Although the chaos theory that evolved from Fichte's thought was based on science and mathematics, the same applications could be applied to history. The patterns, interconnection and repetition elements of chaos theory are one lens to interpret historical events. For instance, the stage was already being set for World War II in 1930, but it was declared when Germany invaded Poland on September 1, 1939. By September 27, 1940, the Empire of Japan joined the war after signing a pact with Germany and Italy.

Not much is written by historians about the Alaska Territorial Guard (ATG) who joined World War II. Despite the lack of historical accounts, it is perhaps worth a look at why the ATG came to be and how it affected one man's life.

The Great Depression began in 1929. The New York Stock Market crashed with runaway trading which resulted in the loss of billions of dollars by investors. Banks were not insured and were unable to pay customers who demanded their money withdrawn. This resulted in more loss of money. People who had lost their money were unable to buy goods or invest. Factories closed. Unemployment was rampant. It proved to be the most severe economic downturn of the century in the United States and Europe, and it lasted until 1939.

Japan, having ended the 700-year-old tradition of rule by shoguns, was reformed under what is known as the Meiji Restoration. Emperor Meiji, during the mid-1800s, worked to westernize Japan and transform the nation into a world power. By 1930, under the reign of Emperor Hirohito, Japan faced a burgeoning population that needed resources and food. The Depression meant a downturn in nations buying goods from Japan's manufacturers. Nationalism swept the globe. The Japanese revived ancient beliefs regarding racial purity and the divine attributes of the emperor. The beliefs were adopted as Japan sought to maintain and expand its role as the dominant power in Asia. Its answer seemed to be military might and imperialistic expansion. Military preparations began against China, and these military actions would lead to war in Manchuria in 1940.

In Russia, Josef Stalin rose to complete control of the communist government in the Soviet Union. In 1930, Stalin began his Five-Year Plan campaign of industrialization to build and strengthen the economy of the Soviet Union. The forced centralization of Russia's agricultural lands during this decade would lead to the Great Purge in the mid-1930s as many "Old Bosheviks" were removed from their farms to be imprisoned or executed. Under the Soviet police state, citizens were imprisoned, impoverished, and executed by the millions.

Unemployment, poverty and homelessness in Germany in 1930 led to political chaos. Under German President Paul von

Hindenburg, the parliament failed to seat a governing majority. Democracy was weakened and elections became frequent. The Nazi, or National Socialist German Worker's Party, seized the opportunity to gain a plurality in the parliament. Adolf Hitler's path to become German Chancellor, and later dictator, was beginning. The horror of World War II in Europe initiated by German nationalism was on the horizon.

In the United States, Americans were reeling from the Stock Market Crash of October 29, 1929. Financial institutions closed, savings were lost, and one quarter of American workers were unemployed. Poverty and homelessness swept the nation in the same way the Dust Bowl would sweep the topsoil off of the mid-western farms in storms. The black storms made planting crops impossible and reached as far as New York. Farmers were displaced. President Herbert Hoover urged Americans to be self-reliant and wait out the economic hardship instead of taking government action to mitigate the economic disaster. The suffering led Americans to seek a new course of action which would result in the election of Franklin D. Roosevelt as president in 1932. Americans waited for help in charity bread and soup lines, lived in shanty towns and struggled to care for their families despite bankruptcies, closed factories and eroded farms. Worst of all, a man could not drown his sorrows in whiskey. The federal prohibition of alcohol sales in America began in 1920 and would only end in 1933.

FURTHER BACK DURING THE 1800S AND early 1900s, gold miners sought their fortunes along the Yukon. The miners were supplied by stern wheels, barges and small steamer ships. 1,980 miles of river flowing from British Columbia across Yukon, Canada into and across interior Alaska to the coast of the Bering Sea earns the title of "The Mighty Yukon." The Yukon is the longest river in Alaska and was the principal means of transportation across the state.

In 1913, gold was discovered along the middle Yukon at what was soon named Wilson Creek. Nearby a boom town blossomed, called Marshall. After the birth of a girl in the mining supply town, the community was called Fortuna's Ledge. The nearby Marshall Landing along the Yukon became a supply town for the Alaska Commercial Company. Over 3,000 gold prospectors, mine workers and their families rushed to the area to grab a piece of the fortune from the earth. A post office, saloon, dance hall, trading post, hotel, church and school were soon part of the boom town. Cabins were built and a bustling industry burgeoned around the many mines in the area. Natives were hired alongside the miners. Employment included woodcutting for building cabins and supplying fuel to the mines. Hunters and fishermen supplied food to supplement the store supplies. Bush pilots began providing transport flights for passengers and supplies. River boat workers helped barge or steamer supplies downriver from the village of Nenana which was connected to the Alaska Railroad.

By 1926, the place's mining activity was winding down and the area's population fell. However, a number of mines remained open and the mining community base stayed on so that a steady modest population remained through 1930. As the influx of miners dwindled by their leaving, the Yupik people flourished in their home villages. Yupik men often worked for the remaining mines to support their families.

The Yupik people were often referred to as Eskimos along with their Inupiaq neighbors to the north in Alaska by non-Native people. The Yupik lived along the Yukon River from Russian Mission to the delta alongthe Bering Sea coast. The name Yupik translates in English to 'real people'. The Yupik lived in the Yukon and Kuskokwim River area of Alaska for thousands of years. The Yupik established a rich culture based on hunting, fishing and gathering. Their culture was based on respect for the land and its resources, which led to an elegant, or efficient and sustaining, subsistence life in harmony with their environment. The Yupik had established centuries of patterns of traditions, interconnections with the land they lived on and repetitions of ceremonies that renewed a religious respect for their land as a natural indigenous expression of chaos theory.

Chapter One

New Life

Aata sat waiting. He stuck his hands in his pockets. He fingered the gold nuggets that were stored in each one. Aata had worked in the gold mines the summer before. He saved the nuggets to sell to the trading store and buy a boat and nets so he could fish for salmon in the summer. His hard work and careful savings had allowed him to prosper. Aata had a family to feed now. He thought about how good life was for him. He loved Aana, his wife. He was overcome with deep love for their unborn child. He smiled to himself as he wondered if the child would be a daughter or son. Then, he took a deep breath and picked up his wood working tools again. He was making a pair of snowshoes.

Other men surrounded Aata in the qasqiq, the men's house. They were working on snowshoes and carvings or other handicrafts of their own. They spoke to Aata and encouraged him as they worked. This encouragement was a positive custom of the Yupik tradition. The men were Yupik men who lived in the village of Tuckchuck along the lower Yukon River in Alaska.

It was February 1930. The weather had been unusually cold beginning since the previous November. The temperatures had dropped to 60 degrees below zero in December and January. However, the cold snap had broken in early February. A warm spell spread over the lower Yukon area as the days were slowly lengthened.

In the ena, the women's house, Aata's wife, Aana, was in labor. She was giving birth to their first child. Yupik women from the village attended her as Aata waited in the men's house. She had gone into labor at midday and now it was early evening.

The elder of the village spoke to Aata. He began an account of the time his son was born. Aata listened to the elder carefully. It was the Yupik way. The experience of the elder would help Aata in his new role as a father.

The evening had barely progressed when a woman appeared in the doorway of the qasqiq. She was smiling. The man had a son, Qetunraq. The mother and baby were sleeping. Both were healthy and strong. She ducked back out of the door. The men congratulated Aata. Aata grinned broadly. His heart swelled as he thought of his first-born son.

THE YEARS PASSED AND QETUNRAQ GREW. He proved to be a quick learner. He was immersed in living his Yupik traditions in his village of Tuckchuck. His parents doted on him. The elders spoiled him. The boy's disposition was bright and cheerful. Qetunraq had a quick smile with deep dimples in both cheeks. He had a profound sense of humor and loved to make people laugh.

Qetunraq's first language was Yupik. Yupik was the only language spoken in his home and village of Tuckchuck. When he was around five years old, he learned a few English phrases when he accompanied Aata to the store upriver in Fortuna Ledge when it was time to sell the furs from trapping over the winter. Qetunraq could follow the English conversations between his father and the white men. However, the boy's thoughts began in Yupik and remained so all his life.

One day, when Qetunraq was only two years old, Aana hugged him tight. She kissed him and held him close as she whispered in his ear, "You are so smart and quick! You are going to be a great nukalpiaq! You are going to be a good hunter and a good provider for your family!"

Qetunraq smiled at his mother's words. It was the first time in the Yupik way, that he became aware of himself. He began to see his mother, Aana, and everyone else as if for the first time. He realized now that he was a person separate from his mother.

Aana's face became serious. There was a melancholy in her eyes. Qetunraq anxiously began to tug on her sleeve. He was wondering what was wrong. His mother gave a sad smile. She whispered that he would leave her. He would leave the Yupik way and live his life far away from Tuckchuck and his village.

Tears welled up in Qetunraq's eyes.

His mother hugged him tight. "You will come home again after many travels." She paused a moment, "Your Yupik ancestors are always with you. The Spirit of the land always remembers you!"

Qetunraq searched her face to try to understand her words.

The mother smiled as she caressed his cheek. "I am here. I love you!"

Qetunraq felt a warm wave of love wash over him. He nestled against his mother and fell asleep.

When Qetunraq turned five, he left his mother and went to the qasqiq to live with the men. The men taught him about hunting, trapping, and everything necessary to the Yupik traditions of living.

When Qetunraq was seven, the Catholic priest came to Tuckchuck. The priest instructed the villagers about the sacraments and Catholic faith. He encouraged the Yupiks to build cabins for individual family homes instead of communal living in the men's or women's houses. The people built cabins for each family, but still gathered in the men's and women's houses for traditional activities and dances.

Elders continued to teach the younger Yupiks in traditional ways. Often, the teaching of important life lessons was through story telling. An elderly grandmother took Qetunraq and the children of the village aside and told them the story of how the crane got its blue eyes. The story impressed the boy and he carried the lesson in his heart all his life.

"A long long long time ago, Crane was hungry. It was autumn. The nights were getting cooler. The Yupiks in their fish camps were finishing their harvest of salmon. Silver salmon were cut and hung on the drying racks. The Yupiks began to think of gathering berries for food for the coming winter. The families packed away the strips of dried salmon. The nights became darker and cooler. In the hills far beyond the Yukon River and on the tundra, it was time for berries to ripen. The blueberries were sweet and abundant.

"Crane had been flying a long time and was tired. He landed on a hill. He could see the bright waters of the Yukon flowing towards the sea below him. Beautiful tundra spread all around him. The evening breeze wafted up the hill as the sun began setting in the west. The breeze carried a sweet fragrance of berries. Crane's stomach growled.

"Crane looked around. He saw berries everywhere! There were blueberries, red cranberries, black crowberries and orange salmonberries. The berries were ripe and juicy. Crane's stomach growled loudly as he stared at the berries.

"Crane decided to pick tasty salmonberries first. Crane had to lean down to pick the berries off the short plants. Crane quickly became annoyed. It was slow picking because he had to keep looking around for foxes or other dangers approaching him on the tundra.

He was so hungry that he wanted to pick faster and fill his stomach.

"Crane looked around. He spied a log and he had an idea. He took his eyes out and set them on the log. He sternly told his eyes to keep a look out for danger. He told them to cry out if they saw danger approaching. His eyes replied that they would obey his command to keep a lookout for danger.

"Crane knelt down and began to feast on the salmonberries. Immediately, his eyes cried out that danger was approaching! Crane raced to the log and put his eyes in. He looked around and saw no danger. His eyes told him to look in the Yukon River far below. Crane squinted. He could see a small log floating by on the river. He told his eyes that it was just a log floating by and not danger. I tried my best to find the correct Yupik words throughout the writing, using my university course study and getting advice to be as accurate as I could be since I did not grow up speaking Yupik.

"Crane set his eyes on the nearby log again. He instructed them to not cry out until they saw real danger. The eyes agreed and apologized for interrupting Crane's dining on berries.

"Crane began to eat voraciously. He moved along the hill further and further from the log. He grabbed beaks of crowberries and blueberries. He moved further and found cranberries. Every berry tasted so good! All Crane thought about was eating until his stomach was nice and full.

Suddenly, Crane paused. He heard his eyes crying for help. The eyes said a fox was taking them! Crane turned around and listened but the cries of his eyes moved further and further away until he could no longer hear them.

"Crane felt around as he tried to find his way. An idea came to him. Berries were round like eyes! He would try to use berries as eyes!

"Crane felt around on the ground. He found crowberries. Crowberries are black and Crane could not see anything when he put them in his eye sockets. Next, Crane found salmonberries. Salmonberries are orange like salmon flesh. Everything looked strangely orange when Crane tried to use the salmon berries for eyes.

Then, Crane put cranberries in his eye sockets. The sky, tundra and river were red. Crane shook his head. Finally, Crane found some blueberries nearby. He put the blueberries in his eye sockets.

"At last! Crane loved his new blueberry eyes! He loved the blue sky, the blues of the tundra hills and the blue waters of the river. Crane looked around but he could not see his eyes so he kept his blueberry eyes. Crane never again took his new eyes out to watch for danger while he ate. He learned his lesson and he never wanted to lose his beautiful blue eyes."

The story of Crane's blue eyes deeply impressed Qetunraq. He often recalled the elder's words and pondered them throughout his life as he studied his life experiences through his Yupik eyes.

Qetunraq continued to grow. He helped his father hunt, fish, trap and build the things they needed to subsist off the land. The boy found listening to the elders easy and loved to learn all he could about everything. When the elders saw the boy listening to them carefully, they were pleased. The Yupik tradition was strong with Qetunraq.

Chapter Two

DEATH
1978

QETUNRAQ, OR SON IN HIS NATIVE Yupik language, had become known by the nickname Sonny when he was a boy. He could feel a change coming. He studied the camp around him carefully. Although he scrutinized the camp, Sonny couldn't figure out what was making him feel uneasy. The man paused a moment and studied the sky. It was his forty-eighth summer. He stood on the bank of Kuigpak, the Yukon River, in Western Alaska. It was August 1978. Sonny frowned.

Sonny's brother-in-law had left earlier in the morning. The brother-in-law was a quiet man who worked tirelessly. In the Yupik tradition, he provided well for his family by hard work. The subsistence harvesting of food and supplies was an endless, careful effort. The man must have risen before the break of dawn to leave in the river boat. He had told Sonny the night before that he was going up the Yukon to Fortuna Ledge to get some more supplies for fish camp. Sonny did not care to go into the busy village of Fortuna Ledge. He preferred the peace of the fish camp and the company of his sister and nephews and nieces. The brother-in-law understood, he quietly added that he would return late that evening.

Sonny listened for a moment after he awakened. He had risen just as dawn was bearing light to the sky. He rose stiffly and left the tent. Dogs lay around the yard still sleeping. They barely raised their heads as he gently replaced the tent door flap behind him.

The air had a chill as camps along the mighty Yukon always did at this time of the waning summer. A few dying cinders lay in the firepit in the yard. The fire in the smokehouse where the drying salmon hung was burning. His brother-in-law must have rebuilt the smokehouse fires before he left. Sonny threw kindling on the fire before filling the charred coffee pot with fresh coffee grinds and water. He set the pot on the grate. Flames curled around the kindling. He reached for larger pieces of wood.

Sonny's younger sister, Nayagaq, slept in the canvas tent with her four young children. Sonny knew in a few hours, the fish camp would be noisy and full of delightful busyness when the children and their mother arose and met the day. He chuckled softly in amusement as he thought of how good it was to hear Yupik spoken by small children. It felt right and peaceful to be back at fish camp.

The coffee pot heated to a rumbling boil quickly. Sonny poured the black steaming liquid into his tin cup. He limped to the wooden bench that sat next to the tent doorway. Sonny's body was worn out. Arthritis had taken over his joints, especially his knees. The decades of grueling physical labor had taken their toll. The right knee was bone on bone under the kneecap. He sipped the hot liquid. It was hot and strong. He leaned back and sighed.

Sonny began to reflect on what was making him uneasy. He knew that he wanted and needed time to think. He had come home. It had been so long since he had come home. Years, no decades, but it felt like a lifetime that he had been away from home.

Sonny closed his eyes. Memories flooded his mind. He could almost see his father and uncle across the yard, getting ready to set the nets for the day. It was August and the silver salmon would be arriving in the Yukon. His mother, Aana, would still be inside the tent. She would be mixing bannock to fry on the fire for breakfast. Kuukuq and Nayagaq, his younger brother and sister, would be asleep in the tent. The dogs from the two dog teams, Aata's team and Sonny's team, would be staked around the outer rim of the yard.

Sonny opened his eyes and drew back to the present moment. Not many Yupiks ran dog teams anymore. They enjoyed the convenience of snow machines to travel in the winter now.

Pain ran down his right leg. Sonny shifted on the hard wood of the bench. He felt so old. He dismissed the pain and smiled as the first rays of the sun rose. The warmth eased the pain throughout his body. He was home. It had been many years, but he was home.

Sonny thought of the years he had spent away from home. It had been exciting, difficult and distracting. He had seen and done so many things in those years away from the Yukon. He had encountered so many different people.

Now, here he sat at fish camp on the Yukon River. It seemed that life on the mighty river had changed little, if at all. His parents, aunts, uncles and many elders had passed on. In Yupik tradition, their names were given to children born in the next generation so that their memory continued. There was a strength and comfort to know that the names of those who had passed on were still spoken among the living today.

Sonny recalled when he was six years old. He had completed his first year of living in the qasgiq with his father, the men and other boys of Tuckchuck. He had helped his father and uncle build a kayak for his uncle. Sonny proved to his father that he could handle the sharp knife and ax to smooth wooden parts of the kayak frame. He helped stretch and sew the skin over the frame.

Aata was pleased with Sonny's ability to learn skills quickly. Aana shared Sonny's progress when she brought food to the qasgiq for her husband and son. She beamed proudly at her son. Sonny's heart swelled under his parent's gaze.

Then it was time for Aana to teach Sonny. All the boys of the village switched places with their sisters. It was an ancient Yupik tradition that was still being followed. The boys went into their mother's house and learned all the skills that the Yupik mothers had been teaching their daughters. Sonny learned to sew, prepare food and cook. He was delighted to show Aana he could do a good job cutting up fish or other food with her woman's knife. The uluaq or woman's knife consisted of curved blade with a wooden or bone handle. The design allowed for efficient and accurate cutting of fish, seals, caribou, rabbits and birds. She was quick to exclaim in delight that her son did a good job with the knife.

The switching of roles between boys and girls gave the Yupiks the ability to help each other when the harshness of the land demanded that everyone work to survive. It also fostered an appreciation of men for the hard work of women and for women the work of men that required strength. Sonny recalled that the elders of the village said that it was the genuine way of living as a Yuk, a Yupik person.

The way of the life that Sonny had known was changed now. The children did not go to live separately in men's or women's houses as he had lived in his early years.

Sonny reflected on the other ways life had changed since his childhood. The Vietnam War had been fought from 1954 and ended in 1973 with US troop withdrawals. The Army had refused to draft him because of his health. However, many young Alaska Native men had served in the far away war and either did not return or returned changed by the horrors they had witnessed.

The Alaska Native Claims Settlement Act was passed in 1971. It had done little to affect Sonny's life. He had enrolled in a regional corporation and a village corporation under the Act. The effects of the Act on Alaska remained to be seen as the corporations struggled to figure out their role in Alaska Native life. The corporate structure was new to the Alaska Natives as they studied and worked hard to establish the businesses. Sonny hoped that the Act would benefit the future for Alaska Native children.

Sonny smiled as he thought of his nephew, the oldest of his sister's children. The young boy was the same age as he had been at fish camp that important year when his life had changed forever. Sonny's nephew had stayed beside him since he arrived back home, listening to his stories, asking questions and following him around everywhere.

A wave of affection swept over Sonny as he sipped more coffee. He loved his nephews and nieces. It felt so warm and loving to hug his sister's children. Their smiles and giggles made him feel like he was truly home. He felt a connection he had not realized he had missed when he looked on the children's rosy cheeks and Yupik eyes.

Sonny winced as his chest began to hurt. He bent forward, almost dropping the cup of hot coffee. A low groan came from his lips. His hand clutched at his chest. He fought the pain off with an iron will. Slowly, his breath returned. He straightened on the bench and took another sip.

Though he fought off the pain in his chest, Sonny could not fight off the memory. Her little face was seared into his mind. His panik, Bun. His baby girl. His only child, a daughter. Tears began to stream down his cheeks. He surrendered to the painful thoughts and let the memory flow.

She was a cuddly bundle on his lap. Sonny tickled her. She giggled. He laughed. Holding his daughter felt so right. He loved her with a love he did not know he could possess. The tears kept falling as Sonny walked through the memory. He put his daughter down from his lap. Sonny had to leave. He had to go to work. The work would take him to another place far away from Bun. The jobs kept him away until at last it was too late. She had left home. She had gone to boarding school at the Mission. He never saw her again.

Sonny wiped his tears. He wondered how she was. He wondered what kind of young woman she had grown to be. Bun would be fifteen years old now. Sonny grimaced as he remembered trying to send her money, gifts, and letters over the years. He could not find a way to connect with Bun. The woman he had married had grown weary of waiting at home for him all those months while he was at work. She moved away, taking his daughter with her. The last he heard, someone said his daughter wanted nothing to do with him. Sonny couldn't believe it. He sought comfort in a whiskey bottle to stop the pain of losing Bun.

Sonny drew a shaky breath. He now knew what had made him uneasy that morning. It was death.

Sonny had come home to die. He fought it off. He needed time. He wanted to stop and think about things before he walked on to his ancestors. He rubbed his eyes with the back of his sleeve and sipped coffee. A sudden calm came over Sonny. He began to remember another time of his life. It was the year he became a nukalpiartaq, a true hunter.

Chapter Three

THE HUNTER
1942

THE BOY STOPPED A MOMENT TO study the sky. It was his 12th summer. He stood on the bank of Kuigpak, the Yukon River, in Western Alaska. It was July, 1942. Sonny frowned. Qetunraq, or son, in his native Yupik language, had earned the nickname Sonny from the man who ran the trading store in the nearby village of Fortuna Ledge. The nickname became the sole name by which he was known to family and friends. He could feel a change coming. He studied the camp around him carefully. Sonny couldn't figure out what was making him feel uneasy.

Neqlivik, or fish camp, was the Sonny's family summer home. When the great king salmon and chum swam up the Yukon River in great numbers, the family set nets to harvest the fish to dry for the winter food. Sonny helped Aata, his father, along with his uncle, set the nets with the boats in the swirling currents. Kiagtaq, or king salmon, weighed fifty or more pounds. They provided rich oily strips when dried or smoked on wooden racks in the talicivik, or fish shed. Nothing was wasted or unused and the salmon provided food for the family as well as their sled dogs through the long cold winter months.

It was late afternoon. The sun was bright. The days were still long in Cher, or July. Mosquitoes buzzed near the alder brush in the shade, hiding from the smoke of the fires around the camp. Aata was with uncle in the boats, checking the nets before putting them out again in the late evening. Kuukuq, Little Brother, was playing with Nayagaq, Little Sister, outside the large white canvas tent. Inside, Aana, Mother, was getting ready to cook supper. The family dogs lay sleeping about the open area around the tent and fire.

Sonny's family had moved to fish camp in June. They worked long hours of hard subsistence activity, netting, cutting and putting up fish. For a month, Sonny woke up, ate and went to work. He fell into bed late at night or early in the morning, exhausted. However a few days ago, Aata smiled. He was pleased. There were plenty of fish for the winter. The days became fun and relaxed. They continued to work hard to harvest chum salmon, but time allowed for stories by the fire and longer sleep. This was Sonny's favorite time at fish camp. This summer was a good one. He had learned how to pilot the motor and steer the boat to set the nets. He could carry heavy loads of fish like the other men. He learned how to wield the ax and saw. He could build a fish rack or repair one by himself.

"Sonny," his father spoke in his quiet way as he stood beside his son, breaking his reverie. "Your uncle and I just saw a bear across the slough. It was a very large black bear. I think it will come around tonight to steal fish. We must be ready."

Sonny looked at his father as excitement was building inside his young heart. The boy knew he had proved his skills with the hunting rifles over the winter. Already, the young boy had a great story told among the villagers about his hunting success. To the Yupik, rifle cartridges were scarce. The bullets, like everything else in the Yupik tools, were never wasted.

One fall in the previous year, Sonny accompanied his father hunting ducks in the sloughs to feed the family. Sonny had smiled as his father guided the bow of the boat towards a flock of ducks. He spied the birds in a tight group and pointed the shotgun. As the loud blast of the shotgun died down, he smiled again as his father laughed! Twelve ducks in one shot!

Sonny had begun his hunting with a feat no one in the village had ever accomplished. He was only eleven then. Now he was twelve and would be expected to help his father and uncle defend the fish camp from the bear. The bear was not only a danger for his family and might steal their hard-earned winter store of salmon, but it would also provide food.

The bear hid in the thick brush along the riverbank during the day. Occasionally, the dogs would sniff the breeze that had heralded evening and barked. The family ate supper and washed. Aana put the younger ones to bed in the tent and settled inside with them.

Sonny went with his father and uncle in the boat. They set the nets in the river for the night. As they returned to the camp, Aata banked the fire in the middle of the yard. He motioned to Uncle and his son. It was decided that they would tie the dogs on the far side of the tent in the thick tall grass there. The dogs would not scare the bear off before the men had a chance to shoot it and still protect the back of the tent where Aana and the younger children slept.

It was agreed that Sonny would sit by the fire with one of the rifles. Uncle would wait and watch by the boats. Aata would keep watch for the bear out of sight beyond the shed. The only way the bear could approach the camp was from the slough and the far end of the camp. In a line, the men faced the slough with their backs to the tent. From their positions, the men had the vantage to see the bear's approach and be clear to shoot their rifles without anyone of them in the line of fire.

The day was turning to the gray dusk of early night when they finished tying the dogs up and took their positions. They stoked the fire, so the corners of the front yard were lighted. Sonny's position was the least likely for the bear to approach. He knew that it was also the most important area to defend because the tent where his mother and younger siblings slept was behind him. The bear was expected to come to the fish shed where Aata could shoot it once the bear topped the riverbank on the near side of the slough.

Sonny waited and watched. At first, his heart pounded. After several long hours, he relaxed. The tent was silent. The dogs had settled in beyond the tent in the tall grass. He could still make out his father on the far end of the yard. Occasionally, Aata would silently swat at a mosquito. Uncle was out of sight in the boats on the river shore below the bank, but he was closer to Sonny than his father was. A star came out in the sky. Sonny studied it. In the long daylight of the arctic summer nights, the stars had hid from sight from May til now.

Then a branch broke! The sound came from the riverbank straight ahead, midway between the yard and the shed. The bear was approaching!

Sonny looked at his father. Aata stiffened up. He leaned forward, peering at the shadowy brush along the top of the riverbank, beyond the shed on the side facing the slough. With measured care, he brought the rifle up and aimed down the sights.

Sonny swung his rifle to his shoulder. He stared at the far end of the yard. There seemed to only be shadows in the grasses and brush. A cold wave washed over the boy as he realized that he had never faced a bear before. His hunting success was highly praised but he had not hunted the most dangerous quarry, the bear. How many times had he listened to the older men tell of hunting bears? Some had faced charging bears and met the danger calmly. It seemed to be the greatest challenge to a hunter to keep his head in the face of a charging bear. He forced himself to breathe evenly. He was a Yupik hunter. The bear was expected to go to the shed to steal the salmon stored inside and his father would be the shooter.

From Sonny's left, he saw his uncle stealthily peeking over the bank. Uncle must have heard the bear too. Sonny knew that his uncle was standing on the bank above the boats in order to see above the top of the rise, but would not move further. The boats smelled strongly of salmon from hauling in the nets and they could not allow the bear to damage the boats. Uncle raised his arm and motioned to Aata. Aata barely moved, still pointing his rifle. It was clear that Aata could now see the bear from his position. Uncle glanced up at Sonny. He gestured towards Aata. The boy nodded and jabbed his rifle towards the direction of the bear. Uncle nodded and disappeared again below the bank.

Long minutes passed. Sonny could not see the bear behind the shed. He watched his father intently. Aata was taut. The barrel of his rifle moved slightly from side to side.

It happened so quickly that Sonny could not think. Bang! Flames shot out from the barrel tip of Aata's rifle! The bear was still out of sight behind the shed as it roared. In a flash, Aata chambered another bullet and shot again.

The bear roared again. It charged around the shed and up the yard towards the fire and tent! Sonny pulled the trigger. BANG! His ears rang. The bear fell on the grass beyond the fire.

Aata and Uncle ran up on either side, ready to fire in case the bear got up. They waited a few minutes before Uncle slowly made his way to the bear and poked it with his gun. He smiled at the others. The bear was dead.

Stunned, Sonny joined his father and uncle standing over the dead bear. The bear was huge! Its mouth was open and its teeth were white in the dusk. "My shots hit it here in the shoulder," Aata was saying. "Your shot hit it here in the heart! You killed it, Sonny!" Aata and Uncle looked at the boy in admiration.

Sonny was trembling with excitement. He had become a real Yupik hunter!

Uncle patted Sonny on the shoulder. "You are now a nukulpiartaq!"

Sonny's heart swelled with happiness. A nukulpiaq was the Yupik word for a strong young man who was a successful provider for his family with good hunting, fishing and trapping. Sonny knew his Aata and Uncle were nukulpiaqs and it was his dream to be one too.

Sonny knew that to be called a nukalpiartaq meant that he was as fine a hunter as his father and uncle, but much younger. The name recognized that Sonny worked hard at his chores and listened carefully to his Aata, Uncle and elders when they taught him the traditions of the Yupik.

Aana and the two smaller children emerged from the tent as the dogs in the grass beyond barked in a loud chorus. Aata built up the yard fire so that it lit up the area. The men began to skin and butcher the bear by the light of the fire.

After admiring the bear, Aana tousled Sonny's hair affectionately, praised him for his shooting skill and bravery. Then she gathered the young ones and returned to bed in the tent. Sonny helped the men as they cared for the bear and helped carry the meat to the shed. After a couple of hours, he sat by the fire a moment. Soon, he was fast asleep.

Aata chuckled. He nudged his son and gently led him to the tent where he fell on the bed and slept soundly.

Chapter Four

THE STORE
1942

TWELVE YEAR OLD SONNY WOKE WITH a start as his stomach growled loudly. As he opened his eyes, Kuukuq pounced on his bed, saying, "Finally, you are awake!" Nayagaq joined her brothers, smiling broadly. The tent was filled with the delicious aroma of freshly fried bread and sizzling meat.

Kuukuq tugged on his brother's arm, "Aana made frybread and she opened the sweet milk!"

In the corner of the large tent stood a flat top wood stove. The fire was roaring as Aana stood over it, cooking. "For my hunter!" she said proudly as she pointed to a plate of pieces of crispy-edged frybread. Next to the bread was a bowl full of sweetened condensed milk for dipping the bread. It was Sonny's favorite treat aside from Aana's agutaq, or Eskimo ice cream. The ice cream consisted of lard or shortening whipped into light fluffiness, mixed with whitefish and berries. Since sweetened condensed milk was store-bought from the merchant in the upriver village of Fortuna Ledge, Sonny knew he was being honored with a special treat for shooting the bear that had raided the fish camp the previous night.

Sonny ate until he was full of fried bread dipped in sweet milk and gulped down tea out of a tin cup. He finished his breakfast, hugged his mother and stepped outside. It was a warm sunny day. The fire in the yard was smoldering. All traces of the bear were gone. The dogs were loose again, sleeping around the yard in the shade. Sonny knew the dogs had enjoyed a good meal from the bear as well.

Kuukuq ran past with Nayagaq on his heels. They ran to the bank where the boats were tied. Sonny followed. He found Aata working on the boat engine. Uncle was loading bundles into the large skiff.

The skiff was constructed by Aata out of plywood and other materials. Aata had bought the outboard motor from the trading post in Fortuna Ledge several years earlier with the fine furs he had trapped. Aata's rifles, ammunition, fishing nets and other supplies were also purchased with furs. Aata was known as a skilled trapper and his hard work provided well for his family. Occasionally, Aata returned to working in the gold mines that remained open around Fortuna Ledge for money to buy supplies.

"We are going to Fortuna Ledge to trade some of the bear for supplies," Aata said as he closed the cover on the outboard motor and cleaned his hands on a rag. "We will take a load of fish home on the way."

Tuckchuck, the family's home village, was less than ten miles below Fortuna Ledge on the Yukon River. Next to their log cabin in Tuckchuck was a food storage shed that was dry and secure as a place to keep their hard-earned harvest for the long winter months. The precious dried salmon would be carefully put in the shed along with the smoked bear meat.

"Are you going to trade the bear hide?" Sonny asked his father.

Aata nodded and smiled at his son proudly. Sonny felt warm inside as he turned and raced back to help his mother carry things to load in the boat. Finally, the boat was loaded. The fires were put out and the dogs were fed again. The family left the dogs loose for the day, planning to return that night.

Sonny whistled loudly and called, "Buddy!" Buddy was Sonny's black and white dog. He was the lead dog for the boy's sled dog team. Sonny had begun helping his father run the trap line two winters earlier. For his hard work on his father's trap line, he earned his beloved sled dogs.

Once, when Buddy was a puppy wriggling in Sonny's arms as the boy sat outside the Fortuna Ledge trading post, the storekeeper walked by. The white man was tall and loud, but friendly and jovial. He spied the puppy, extended a hand to scratch his ears, and said loudly, "Hi there, Buddy!" He laughed and smiled at Sonny, "That's a good dog! He's going to be your team leader!" From that day on, the dog answered to Buddy. He proved to be a fine dog.

Sonny nestled in the bow of the riverboat with his arms around Buddy. Aana was curled up with the younger ones comfortably settled on a caribou hide. Aata stood at the motor as Uncle pushed the boat off the bank and nimbly leapt in. Aata started the motor and after it warmed up, the family began the journey upriver to Tuckchuck to store the salmon at their home. Then, they planned to continue upriver to Fortuna Ledge to trade the bear meat at the trading post for supplies.

Tuckchuck was deserted as the family arrived. The villagers were at their individual family fish camps along the Yukon. After quickly storing the load in the food shed, the family continued on to Fortuna Ledge. The shore of the river near Fortuna Ledge was full of boats beached up on the landing. The family wondered why so many people were there. Shouldn't they be out at fish camp?

It was almost August. August was berry picking season. Blueberries, salmonberries, blackberries, and cranberries would be harvested by families in their traditional berry picking patches along the hills up and down the Yukon. Berries were an important part of the Yupik diet and were stored in the shed for winter months.

The family pulled into shore. Buddy leapt off the boat and followed Sonny closely. Uncle, Aata and Sonny carried their loads to the mercantile while Aana towed the younger ones down the dusty street by each hand. The children shyly walked along with large eyes taking in all the bustle of Fortuna Ledge. There was a crowd of Yupik at the merchant's.

The trader was flushed and talking loudly to the people gathered. He saw Aata and waved him into the store. As Aata spoke with the trader, Sonny listened. He knew some English but strained to follow the storeowner's flood of words. The man was talking about war. He said the Japanese had invaded the Aleutian Islands of Attu, Kiska and Adak along the coast of Alaska. Earlier in June, the Japanese had bombed Dutch Harbor. There was much alarm and fear that the Japanese would bomb and invade mainland Alaska.

The trader eagerly accepted Aata's bear hide. He packed supplies for the family to take home. Then, he retrieved a shiny box from the shelf behind the counter. "Take this, Aata. It is a radio. Listen to the news. You will want to know if the Japanese invade the Yukon River."

He showed Aata how to turn on the radio and tune it to the news. He opened the battery compartment and shared how to change the batteries. "Here are some extra batteries. They should last you until you come in next time." Aata seemed unsure. The trader insisted and said the radio was paid with the supplies by the bear hide.

The storekeeper went on, "The Japanese are a threat to all of us! You need to listen to that radio and hear the news. The Japanese have been stealing our salmon from the Bering Sea at the mouth of the Yukon for years! They sail up Bristol Bay with their boats and nets, and they don't care about leaving any salmon for the people up the Yukon who need those fish to eat all winter.

"The Japanese have submarines along the coast! They fly their planes over the whole coast of Alaska and even further inland than Fortuna Ledge! Our country is at war with Japan. We have to be ready. They could come up the Yukon and enslave us all. Then, they would take the women and children. They took the women and children off of Attu and Adak and took them back to Japan."

The man paused to take a deep breath as he shook his head in concern. "The radio will help you know what is going on. This war with Japan is a little too close to home for us here in Alaska. We need good men like you to be informed about what is going on. We need leaders like you to know what to do if those Japanese come invading."

"Quyana," Aata thanked the man solemnly and carried his goods outside. Sonny followed him with Buddy at his heels. Aata called to Aana who was waiting outside the store while talking with women from the Fortuna Ledge. She saw the concerned look on Aata's face and called her two young ones to follow. They walked to the riverbank in silence.

When they reached the boat, Uncle was waiting with a group of village men. He was excited. "A plane is coming!" he said.

Chapter Five

THE MAJOR

THE 5ᵗʰ OF JANUARY, 1930 WAS bitterly cold. The men, rough and burly from working in the gold mines of Canada's North, raised their whiskey glasses and sang. Marvin Marston smiled as he nodded to the happy birthday wishes. He sipped his whiskey slowly and set his glass down thoughtfully. It was an accomplishment to reach the age of forty-one years.

The bartender, Perron, filled the shot glasses of five men at the table as he laughed. The celebration of a birthday in the middle of winter, especially in the gold mining town of Pascalis, Quebec, Canada, was a welcome one. The men had been working long hard hours mining gold in the nearby Cournor Mine. Pascalis was booming. It was the gold that these hearty men wrought with their sweat and might that attracted thousands of fortune seekers. The Cadillac gold belt in the Abitibi region of northern Quebec was full of gold and precious minerals. Four mines, including Cournor, were worked by ambitious men in the boom community of Pascalis.

In the early morning hours, Marvin Marston bid Perron good night and stepped outside of the large wooden building that was the center of Pascalis. The northern lights were dancing across the sky. He pulled his fur coat tighter over his woolen shirt and pants. He paused a moment to enjoy the aurora borealis with a broad grin on his face. Life was good here. A man could drink whiskey to celebrate unlike back in his home in Tyler, Washington in the United States. There was wild beauty all around. Marston loved the arctic, the hard work and the boisterous people of Quebec's gold mining industry. A man could not find a job in the States, where a quarter of men languished without work or income.

Later, Marston lay in his bed at the mining workers' quarters. He reflected on his life. Marvin Marston's childhood home was a sturdy homestead cabin in eastern Washington State. After five years at Tyler, Marston's father drove the family to Seattle for a better life. Marston chuckled to himself as he recalled the dusty ride to the city on the coast in the horse drawn wagon. As he grew, he worked horses and bulls. He had gone to Alaska on a steamer and worked as a longshoreman. Marston's journey had led him to high school, college and the National Guard in Seattle. He had attended college in Illinois and served in the National Guard there. Various business ventures in land development had led him from coast to coast. Now, steady profitable work was his in the gold mines of Quebec, Canada.

Marston concluded his life was exciting and full of adventure which is just how he liked it. Despite the Depression, the Dust Bowl storms, and the Prohibition in the States, a man could make a good life for himself if he worked hard and followed opportunities.

Marston's musing turned towards Alaska. He envisioned the gold miners of Nome. As a teenager, he had worked on a steamer that brought supplies to the gold miners of Nome. Then, his mind was made up. He would finish a few more gold mining seasons in Quebec, earn a savings to move on and return to Nome. A fortune awaited him in Alaska, he was sure of it. He turned on his side, pulled the heavy blankets tight and fell asleep in the conviction that the future was bright for Marvin Marston.

What he did not know at the time was how he would actually return to Alaska. He would join the Army. The Territorial Governor of Alaska, Ernest Gruening, would appoint Marston to organize the Alaska Territorial Guard. He would earn the nickname "Muktuk" as he drove dog teams across the remotest parts of northern and western Alaska to recruit and train Alaskan Native men and women of all ages to serve in the Guard to protect the United States territory from the Japanese attacks. Muktuk Marston's belief in the abilities of the indigenous people as a military force in the remoteness of Alaska would lead to the protection of the territory and influence the lives of many native people who served. The strong relationship with the land inspired in the Yupik people of all ages became a strength to readily join the Alaska Territorial Guard in order to protect the land from the Japanese invasion when recruited by Muktuk Marston.

1942

SONNY LOOKED AROUND HIM AS HE stood above the landing on the Yukon riverbank. He recognized faces in the crowded villagers. It appeared everyone from Tuckchuck was present in Fortuna Ledge. Everyone in Fortuna Ledge and the nearby villages up river were also standing along the river. Children played. Dogs barked. Buddy occasionally growled from his station at Sonny's feet. Women were chatting in Yupik as the men stared at the sky silently. The white postmaster, teachers and storekeepers all joined the villagers as they waited. After a time, everyone fell silent. Ears strained as they listened for the hum of a plane's engine approaching.

It was past afternoon and the early evening was approaching. In late July 1942, the arctic white nights were reserved and despite the gloaming, the sun was warm as it sank in the sky and the wind was calm. The waiting crowd began to fidget. The postmaster mumbled something and left to his cabin. After long minutes passed, the hum sounded!

The villagers murmured and peered at the sky. Finally, Uncle shouted, "There it is!" A speck appeared in the sky to the south. It was the approaching airplane. The Major was coming!

The plane circled the village once before descending to its landing approach along the river. The pontoons skimmed the calm surface of the mighty placid river until at last, the plane beached at the river bank. A man opened the door of the aircraft and hopped down onto a float. He tossed a rope to Aata, who was waiting on the shore. Aata pulled the rope until the plane was safely secured on the bank. The man jumped off the float and shook Aata's hand firmly. He smiled and waved at the crowd above him on the banks of the river. The man waited to extend a hand in assistance to two other men exiting the plane. The trio climbed up the bank and greeted the villagers.

"Hello! Hello! I am Major Muktuk Marston!" The crowd laughed at the name Muktuk. The man smiled. "This is your Governor, Alaska Territorial Governor Ernest Gruening!" The Major turned to Aata. "Is there a kashim where we can assemble everyone?"

Aata replied that there was a dance hall that also served as a community hall. He nodded and began leading the way.

The crowd followed the men to the hall.

Sonny followed the crowd. He wondered how the stranger knew about kashims. There was one in Tuckchuck. It was also called the qasqiq, or men's house. This house was built for a gathering place for men to live in and work on various projects. Since it was large enough for the entire village, it was also used for yuraq, or Yupik dancing, and other ceremonies.

After the villagers and their visitors were all inside the dance hall, the Governor moved to the center and addressed the Yupik. "Thank you for welcoming us here. My fellow Alaskans, my fellow citizens of the United States of America, I need your help. The President of our great nation needs your help. We are at war. Japan attacked our Navy at Pearl Harbor, Hawaii without warning. Then, Japan attacked our Aleutian Islands. We must be ready if the Japanese attack mainland Alaska. The Major will explain to you how you can help protect your homes, your villages, Alaska and our nation." The Governor moved aside and waved the Major up to speak.

The Major stood up in the center. "I have to speak to you about something very important. It is so important that I have to come right to the point and take care of the business I am here for enlisting your help to protect our land without delay. We have to keep flying on to other villages, so we leave here today as soon as we are finished. But first, let me explain one thing. I *earned* the name Muktuk." The villagers laughed politely. Muktuk is the Eskimo word for whale blubber, the whale fat from bowhead whales that is an Eskimo delicacy eaten raw. How could a white man be named Muktuk?

"An Inupiaq man in Nome challenged me. He said he could beat me in a muktuk eating challenge! Well, I beat him. So I earned my name!" The major smiled. The Yupik laughed again. Then he grew serious. "We are at war with the Japanese! The Japanese are not going to invade and kill just gussaqs or white men. They will kill you too. The Japanese will shoot you, or enslave you, and take your women and children. They will kill off the animals you hunt and steal the fish you need to feed your families all winter. They will bomb you. They attack without warning with their bombs and planes!"

The Major continued. "We need your help. We need you to become soldiers, members of the Alaska Territorial Guard. We need you to guard your villages.

"Our currently enlisted territorial guard has been deployed to help in the Lower 48 with protecting the West Coast from the Japanese. Our army soldiers are few and stretched thin. They do not know the land like you do. They do not know how to survive in the winter like you do. They do not know how to travel or camp or find food to eat to survive like you do. We need you. We will supply you with rifles and ammunition. We will provide uniforms. We will give you radios to call and give regular scouting reports to our Army base in Nome. You can call on the radio and report to us if the Japanese are flying over in their planes or if they are landing in their warships or submarines. Then we can send our bombers to help you fight to stop the Japanese from coming any further.

"Will you fight? We just came from Bethel and before that, we traveled to other villages. The people of Bethel, Hooper Bay, Mekoryuk and Quinhagak are all signed up. Are you willing to practice, scout and shoot the Japanese if you see them?

"We will appoint a chain of command for your village. There will be an appointed officer to be in charge of your Guard unit. I will give him a manual of arms. You will do drills with the rifles. Each Guardsman will know how to clean and maintain his rifle and take care of his ammunition.

"You will put together a plan for your village and assign tasks to each guard. Some of you will keep trails open. Some of you will keep watch on the skies for spy balloons or planes. Some of you will help make maps of trails and help the Army learn the best ways to travel through the country here. Some of you will build cabins along those trails for our Army to camp in bad weather. Some of you will need to stash rations and supplies along the trails for our Army to use. You will learn care for the wounded and dress wounds."

The Major paused and looked at the men. "Will you help?"

Sonny's heart swelled with pride as Aata stood up. Aata spoke clearly, "Yes, I help." Uncle joined him. Sonny hurried to their sides.

As each of the village men, from the oldest to the young boys, rose to answer that they would join the Guard, the Major smiled. "I have a paper for you to sign." He held up a sheet of paper. "It is the Alaska Territorial Guard Oath and Certificate of Enrollment. You will sign it and then we will recite the oath together."

A young woman spoke up. "Can women join?" Everyone turned to her in surprise. They waited for the Major to answer.

The Major nodded. "Yes. Some of the women in Bethel are going to train to be nurses. They are going to build and work in a hospital to care for wounded soldiers in Nome." He chuckled. "Do you know how to do carpentry to help build the hospital?" The woman smiled and stood up. She wanted to sign up.

The woman and men filed forward. Each of the volunteers signed the paper and gathered to the side, waiting to say the oath together.

When it was finally Sonny's turn, the Major studied him. "How old are you, son? Do you know how to shoot a rifle?"

The men from the villages broke into laughter.

"He just shot the biggest black bear I ever saw! He killed it while it charged with one shot to the heart!" the storekeeper said. "He may look young, but he is the sharpshooting soldier you want, Major!"

The Major smiled and nodded approvingly.

After everyone signed the paper, the Major stood and read the oath. As the men repeated it, the Governor nodded. The men and one woman of Fortuna Ledge and Tuckchuck were officially Alaska Territorial Guard members!

Chapter Six

Drills

1942

Forty-one men from the village of Tuckchuck had signed up to become Guards. Captains and lieutenants were appointed for each village by the Major. Uncle was captain and Aata was lieutenant. Uncle was given a manual of arms. A radio each was given to Uncle and Aata. The Major promised that Enfield rifles for each man and ammunition would be flown in to Tuckchuck by plane in the coming weeks. The uniforms would come by winter.

After instructions were given to the captains of Fortuna Ledge and Tuckchuck, the Major and Governor left on the plane to enlist other Yupiks in nearby villages. The Governor had explained that Native men and women from all over Alaska were signing up for the Territorial Guard. He added that the Guards along the rivers and coasts of Alaska were the most important for protecting Alaska from the invading enemy.

As Sonny watched the plane lift off the river and bank over the village on its way south, he felt strange. Life had changed. The family solemnly said farewell to the villagers and began their boat ride home. Aana rode in the boat with an arm around both Kuukuq and Nayagaq who fell asleep. Sonny met her gaze. He could see pride and concern in her eyes. She smiled. He smiled back, feeling butterflies in his stomach as he stroked Buddy's fur all the way home. Would he have to shoot the Japanese?

The fall months passed quickly. Sonny and his family were too busy to ponder life. After the Major's visit, Aata and Uncle decided to hurriedly return to fish camp before the rifles arrived and Guard practice drills began. They would work hard to catch and put up as many chum salmon as they could before closing the camp down for the winter. Aata was happy that they had plenty of king salmon already prepared for the coming winter.

Fall time was important for the Yupik people for berry picking and hunting for winter food before the snows and cold weather arrived. Each family had a traditional berry picking area. They traveled by boat to the place when the berries were ripe. Later, the men would go on hunting trips. The time to hunt and pick berries would be shortened by the addition of drills and duties of the Guard. When the family went berry picking, each family member worked hard to gather enough for the winter. The villagers were grateful that it was an abundant year and enough winter food could be stored in less time than in past years.

The planeload of rifles, ammunition and uniforms finally arrived. Uncle distributed the supplies as the men of Tuckchuck lined up. Sonny admired the Enfield rifle that was handed to him. He stared at the ammunition. He had never seen so many bullets. The uniforms were long jackets with patches on the shoulder. There were hats and helmets. Uncle read the patch, "Alaska Territorial Guard." The men gave a low whistle. They were officially soldiers.

Uncle had studied the manual of arms. He led the men in drills. Sonny and the others learned quickly. The men stood in rows, moving the rifles in unison. They marched around the village in formation. The men practiced with the rifles. They cleaned the

Enfields carefully and made sure the ammunition was counted and carefully stored.

The men held long discussions. Assignments were made. Some would make up maps of the trails across the land to show the Army where it was best to travel. Others would patrol the river near Tuckchuck. They would meet with neighboring village patrols and keep updated on what was happening on the Yukon River. Uncle would radio reports to the Army in Nome regularly.

Everyone was trained to take care of wounded soldiers. They practiced bandaging and splinting. Stretchers were cut from small trees and canvas was laced on to carry the wounded. The men planned how to handle a plane crash in the area. The map would be consulted and the crash reported on the radio while a team of men would carefully approach the plane. They learned how to distinguish enemy planes from Army planes. Trails were mapped with copies sent to Nome to share with the Army. The men decided where cabins and shelters should be built so they could provide shelter in the harsh weather. The Tuckchuck Guard was trained and organized when the snow finally fell.

Sonny followed the drills with all his might. He kept up with the men. His Enfield was kept shiny and well oiled. He was the best marksman in the Tuckchuck Guard. He kept the rifle with him all the time. He carried the ammunition with care and counted it every night to make sure it was all there.

Aata made a wooden shelf in the family cabin in Tuckchuck. He placed the radio from the store in Fortuna Ledge on it. Every night, after the hard work of the day and the family evening meal, Aata tuned the radio to the news. The family listened. The war was being fought against the far away countries of Germany and Italy. It was also being fought in Alaska.

As an Alaska Territorial Guard lieutenant, Aata had been assigned a radio from the Army. He learned how to send and receive on the set, which he kept on the new shelf next to the store radio. Aata took turns with Uncle making reports to the Army in

Nome. Every other week, he radioed the Commander and gave a short report. Sonny and the other children stood in silence, staring in wonder as their father gave his report. Aata turned the knobs and held the mic in his hand. At first, it was astonishing to hear the strange voice speaking in reply to Aata.

After several months, Aata called Sonny. He lifted down the radio and told his son, "I am going to teach you how to give reports. Learn how to use the radio so you know how to call the Army in case there is an emergency."

Sonny's hands were shaking. He was torn inside. Fear at the thought of Aata not being able to call the Army himself fought with a thrill of being entrusted with the duties of a lieutenant in the Guard! Aata saw his son's nervousness and whispered, "It's okay, son. Be strong." Sonny pursed his lips and listened carefully. He turned the knobs and flicked the switches. He held the mic to his lips and spoke the call signs. He released the call button and waited.

A voice cackled over the radio. It was the Army station in Nome! Sonny gave the update that all was well and no enemy had been sighted. The voice thanked him and signed off. Sonny signed off and handed the mic to Aata. Aata chuckled. "Good job!"

Sonny breathed easier. He felt a sense of relief wash over him. If Aata or Uncle, Tuckchuck or any other village needed help from the Army, he knew what to do. He knew how to call on the radio for help. The war seemed less dangerous and the enemy seemed less terrifying. The Guards were part of the Army. A team could overcome any danger.

Sonny shook his head as he sat on the bench at fish camp. It seemed so long ago when Muktuk Marston signed the men of Tuckchuck up for the Guard.

Chapter Seven

The Balloon

WINTER ARRIVED IN EARLY OCTOBER, 1942. The men of Tuckchuck continued to practice drills for marksmanship and marching. They wore long white coats issued by the Army to blend in with the snow.

The war seemed to fade into the shadows of the long dark days of winter. The Guard heard occasional reports of fighting in the Aleutians. Japanese submarines and warships were spotted off the coast far away. When a plane flew over Tuckchuck, Uncle ran out with his binoculars to see if it was a Japanese invader flying over. Aata had also been issued binoculars, which he kept safe in a case. He took the case with him whenever he went outdoors.

Life became a rhythm like it had been before. They busied themselves with the demands of winter, though the thought of the Japanese enemies lingered in the back of the men's minds.

As the cold weather continued, the river froze. A large area of the Yukon River and tundra between Tuckchuck and the nearest villages was assigned to the men to patrol. Using snowshoes and dog teams, the Guards kept the trails open for travel in the snow. They kept the shelters and caches cleared of snow and stocked with firewood.

The men of Tuckchuck met and decided that they would continue running their trap lines for the winter. They arranged for shifts. The men who traveled the trails to their traps would keep the trails open in that area. Aata was pleased because he was a successful trapper. He supported his family well by trading the high-quality furs he harvested over the winter. Each spring, he loaded the furs to sell or trade in Fortuna Ledge.

Sonny had learned everything from Aata about trapping. Through his own trapping success, the previous year, he had enough furs to buy dogs and a sled. He now had his own dog team. Aata was very proud of him. This winter, Sonny was excited to trap and help the Guards maintain the winter trails.

In late October, Aata told twelve year old Sonny to join him at the qasgiq. Sonny entered the men's house after he had done his chores of feeding the dogs and chopping wood for the house. It was early evening and the room was pleasantly warm. He shed his heavy parka and mittens.

On the wooden platform at the front of the qasgiq, Aata and several other men sat. There was a pile of wood, rawhide and tools. It was time to make a new pair of snowshoes! It was the first time Sonny made his own pair of snowshoes. His old pair of snowshoes was now too small in size, fit for a younger boy.

As Sonny sat down next to Aata, he picked up a long wooden pole. Aata patiently showed him how to peel the bark off and trim the pole into a four sided length. The ends were carefully lashed together. The bow in the middle of the bent pole was the tip of the snowshoe. The lashed ends were the back end of the snowshoe. Then, rawhide laces were intertwined over the space of the curved wood to make the woven interior. The woven rawhide spread the weight of the wearer over a large area and enabled him to walk on the top of the snow without sinking in deeply. Weaving the rawhide had to be done carefully so that a toe hole was open. The toe hole allowed the wearer's foot to lift up and down easily without tripping on the bow of the snowshoes. The long elliptical shape of the snowshoe allowed the wearer to shuffle in the shoes and avoid tripping.

In the Yupik tradition, Sonny worked hard with measured care. As in all things, he watched Aata carefully, listened closely and tried his very best to do the same task as well as his father did. In this way, he had learned to shoot and take care of a gun, which was one of the Yupik men's most important possessions. In this way, he had learned about the land, the weather, the animals and fish. In this way, Sonny made his first pair of snowshoes. It was the same way Sonny learned the stories, dances, songs and traditions of the Tuckchuck elders. He loved to learn and doing things well came easily to him. He felt proud when he stood with the other men of Tuckchuck, especially as a fellow Guard.

Sonny's new snowshoes were finally finished and ready to use. Now the weather had turned extremely cold. The snow was deeper this winter than it had been in the past several years. Sonny would have to use his snowshoes whenever he traveled this winter. The Tuckchuck men worked hard to keep the trails open in the deep snow. They had to go out on patrol more often to keep the snow from accumulating and bogging the dog teams down.

At last, the skies cleared and the temperatures dropped to -40 degrees Fahrenheit at night, but it warmed to a wan 10 degrees in the short sunny part of the day. The snow became crunchy and crystalline.

Sonny knew that the cold weather would cause the fur on the animals he and his father trapped to become luxuriantly thick. When it came time for him to patrol the trail with Aata, he was ready.

Sonny drove his dog team a ways behind his father's team to keep the dogs from tangling and fighting. His dog sled was piled with hides, blankets and provisions. Some of the load would be left at the two cabins along the trail. The rest was the food and gear they needed for their four day patrol. Aata's sled on the other hand was light and ready to be piled high with the animals they harvested from their traps.

The dogs were eager to trot. The sleds raced over the frozen trail. Aata and Sonny wore their white Guard overcoats with their Enfield rifles slung over their backs. Warm fur pants and coats kept them comfortable as the sleds pushed forward through the chilly air. Fur ruffs on their parka hoods kept their faces from freezing. They packed ample ammunition in their pockets and in the sleds. Aata had packed his hunting rifles in his sled for extra protection. He was also ready for any opportunity to hunt animals for food.

The trail left Tuckchuck and crossed the Yukon River. On the eastern bank, the trail rose over the riverbank and onto the tundra. Then, the trail climbed some gentle hills. Beyond the hills, the trail wound on for many miles. Stands of spruce trees edged the frozen lakes on the tundra. As the trail crossed further, the tree stands became larger.

It was 20 miles to the first cabin. The sun had set hours before they reached the tiny wooden structure. The stars were bright and a half moon provided light to travel by.

Sonny helped unload supplies from his sled. Aata lit a fire to cook on and heat the cabin. Sonny fed the two dog teams and made sure the dogs were comfortably settled for the night. They ate in silence. When he nestled in his caribou blankets, Sonny fell asleep immediately.

Aata was starting a fire when Sonny awoke. The cabin was frigid. Soon, the fire warmed the tiny room. Aata handed Sonny a cup of steaming tea. They ate a light meal. As they packed their sleds with their blankets, the dogs ate dried fish and bear fat.

The sun had not risen. It only shone for a few hours each day. The light of dawn reflected off the white snowy ground and it was easy to see, even without the sun. The dogs happily pulled the sleds on down the trail.

It was another 20 miles to the second cabin. The trail continued many miles across the tundra towards the next big river, the Kuskokwim. Aata's trap line ran 10 miles past the second cabin. They would check the traps then return home.

Aata and Sonny reached the cabin in the late evening of their second day on the trail. The following morning, they checked the traps. Every trap had a fine catch of wolverines, lynx or wolves. The sleds were loaded with the animals as they turned towards home.

Sonny had hunted grouse and rabbits with Aata's .22 caliber rifle for fresh meat for the village. Pleased, father and son began the journey home. They planned to travel late until they reached the first cabin. They would spend the last night on the trail and reach home the following day.

After the sun set, the twilight was reflected off the snow. As the evening passed, it became quite dark. The shadows of the spruce stands and tundra brush were inky black. Then overhead the northern lights began to dance brilliantly!

Aata woke early. He was eager to get home. The fire wakened Sonny. After eating and feeding the dogs, they began along the trail back to Tuckchuck. It was gray out as the northern lights had now faded and it would be hours before the sun rose. The dogs pulled forward as they did not need light to follow the trail home.

The sun rose after they had traveled 15 miles. The trail was winding up the back side of the hills before descending down to the Yukon. The dogs slowed as they labored up the hills, but they pulled steadily.

Aata shouted and stepped on the brake of his dog sled. His dog team stopped in bewilderment. Sonny quickly brought his dog team to a halt and set the brake. He walked around his sled, telling his dogs to stay as he walked forward to his father. Aata pulled something from the top of his sled load and began walking back to meet his son.

"Look!" Aata said as he pointed at the sky. Sonny stared. A large silver object was floating through the air! It drifted slowly from the south and was moving up over the hills beyond them.

Aata had his binoculars. He studied the object a moment. Then, he thrust the binoculars into his son's hands and pulled out his Enfield rifle. "It's a Japanese balloon! Quick! Help me shoot it down!" Aata aimed his rifle at the balloon and pulled the trigger. The shot rang out across the face of the hills. The dogs began to bark and howl.

Sonny remembered that the Guard had been warned that the Japanese were sending balloons over Alaska and the West Coast of the United States. The Japanese placed bombs under the balloons. The bombs would explode when the balloon landed.

Uncle had a picture of the balloons that carried bombs. The Guards memorized the pictures of the balloons in case they had to shoot one down. Sonny saw that the object in the sky was the same as the picture Uncle had shown the men at the drill practice. Uncle had said to shoot it down immediately. Sonny shouldered his Enfield and aimed.

After Aata and Sonny shot the balloon several times, it began to sink. It fell to the ground up the hill from them. Aata and Sonny waited. They expected to see the bomb explode. After a long moment, Aata went to his dog team and began up the trail. Sonny ran back to his dog team and pulled the brake. He yelled to his dog team. They followed his father up the hill.

As the trail topped the crest of the hill, they found the balloon. It was a hundred yards off the trail on top of the deep snow. It lay sprawled with its shiny material over the snow's surface. The bottom of the balloon was sunk in the snow. The bomb had not gone off.

"It doesn't look like the bomb is going to explode." Aata said as he studied the object. He thought for a moment before turning to Sonny. "Your dog team is the fastest and your sled is smaller than mine, so it is faster. We will take most of your sled's load and put it on mine. I need you to go back to Tuckchuck as fast as you can and tell Uncle. If you can't find Uncle, call the Army on the radio. Tell them we shot down a Japanese balloon!"

Sonny nodded. He helped Aata unload his sled. He carefully led his dog team past Aata's on the trail to the front so no dogs could fight or get tangled in the harness. He paused as he stood on the sled and looked back at Aata.

"Hurry! Tell Uncle!" Aata urged him.

"Mush!" Sonny shouted to his dogs. The team raced ahead on the trail. He tried not to worry about leaving Aata behind.

At last, Sonny pulled into Tuckchuck. He parked his dog team at his cabin. He jammed the brake into the snow to secure the sled. The dogs lay wearily in their harnesses. Sonny sprinted towards Uncle's cabin. His heart fell as he saw it was dark and quiet. A nearby villager explained that Uncle had taken his family to Fortuna Ledge earlier that day and had not returned yet.

Sonny ran to his home. Aana looked up startled as he burst in the door. She put her fingers to her lips and pointed to his brother and sister already asleep in bed. He was breathless as he went to the shelf and reached the radio down. Aana rose in alarm. "Where's Aata?"

Sonny quickly told his mother as he turned the dials on the radio. "He's coming behind me." He spoke into the mic and called the Army at Nome. "We shot down a Japanese balloon on the Kuskokwim Trail. It landed on top of the hills!"

The soldier questioned Sonny at length. He explained everything. The soldier thanked him and asked him to tell Aata to call him when he arrived.

Aata arrived wearily several hours later. Sonny helped him unharness and feed the dogs. He unloaded the sled as Aata ate and called the Nome Army base on the radio.

As Sonny lay in bed that night, he couldn't sleep. The Japanese had sent a bomb balloon from far away to his homeland. The war had become a reality. He clenched his fists under the blanket as he thought of his mother and the younger children. He would be the best Guard he needed to be to protect his family.

Chapter Eight

SKY WATCH
1943

SEVERAL WEEKS AFTER SONNY AND AATA had shot the balloon down, the Army in Nome sent soldiers to retrieve it. The plane landed on the Yukon River in front of Fortuna Ledge. The Guards of the village had prepared dog teams for the soldiers to take them to the hill where the balloon had been still lay on the snow.

The Guards of Tuckchuck traveled by dog sled to Fortuna Ledge to join the men of Fortuna Ledge as they greeted the Army soldiers from Nome. When the Army Sergeant arrived with his squadron, he asked to speak to the Guards who had shot the balloon down.

Aata and Sonny stepped forward and saluted. Aata gave an account of what had happened on the trail and how they had shot the balloon down. He pointed out that there was no explosion.

The Sergeant listened carefully. He asked Sonny, "Aren't you a little young to be a soldier?"

Aata and Uncle quickly spoke and explained how well Sonny

could shoot. They said he was one of the best Guards. Sonny felt a burst of pride inside. The Sergeant nodded in approval.

The next day, the Army recovered the balloon. The bomb was nowhere to be found. The Sergeant said he thought it might have fallen off somewhere over the ocean or a remote part of the land. It was a good thing. The bomb could have killed anyone who was near where it fell.

A meeting was called in the community hall for the Guard of both Fortuna Ledge and Tuckchuck. The soldiers gave a training talk for the villagers.

The Sergeant explained that a very important war effort was now taking place. It was called the Lend Lease program. In 1941, the previous year, the United States had passed an Act of Congress that approved the lending and leasing of military equipment to other friendly nations fighting in the war.

Alaska's neighbor to the west was the Soviet Union or the USSR. The USSR had been fighting against Germany in Europe. They were running short of supplies to fight the Germans. Although, the USSR was a friend of Japan, the United States decided to help them with military planes. The Soviet Union needed the bombers to win against Germany.

The safest way to fly the planes to the Soviet Union was through Alaska. The planes were flown from the manufacturer in the Midwest United States. They were flown northwest to Edmonton, Alberta, Canada. Then, the planes were taken to an Air Force base near Fairbanks, Alaska.

The pilots from the Soviet Union had a training center on the Air Force Base near Fairbanks. When the planes arrived, the Soviet pilots trained for five days to fly the planes. Then, the pilots flew them to the Soviet Union from Alaska. Sometimes, the pilots landed in Nome, especially if the weather was bad.

The flight path of the planes leaving Fairbanks on their way to the Soviet Union was usually north of Tuckchuck. The Army Sergeant from Nome wanted to train the Guards from Fortuna

Ledge and Tuckchuck to spot the planes. He taught them how to recognize the planes. The Guards learned what to do if a plane went missing and how to search for it. They practiced first aid in case they found an injured pilot.

The Sergeant repeated how important it was that the planes were safe from the Japanese. He stayed three days in Fortuna Ledge and trained the Guards. They went through their drills again and again until the Sergeant was satisfied.

The Sergeant and his soldiers left Fortuna Ledge in the plane back to Nome. They took the balloon with them so they could study it. He nodded goodbye and saluted. Sonny stood tall with his fellow Yupik Guards and saluted back.

After the men returned to Tuckchuck, Uncle called a meeting of the Guard in the qasgiq. He suggested that the men extend their patrol area to the north of the Yukon River along ancient hunting trails. The greater distance that the men covered would help keep watch for the planes being flown from Fairbanks to Nome.

The discussion went late into the night. Many men talked about the disruption that being a Guard had caused to their traditional Yupik way of life. Ceremonies, dances and observations of seasonal practices had been shortened or put aside. Hunting seasons had been cut short or not followed at all, such as hunting for geese, swans or ducks in the fall. Winter fishing for eels, black fish or lush fish had been put aside for military drills and patrols.

Aata listened carefully to each man's concern. He stood up and addressed the men. He suggested a two-week delay in lengthening the patrols. The patrols that the Guards had been carrying out would continue by rotating teams. The rest of the Guards were free to do activities for their families. In two weeks, it would be Christmas. A Catholic priest would come by dog team to say Mass in the village. It was a time of solemn celebration. Two weeks later, the Russian Orthodox priest would arrive to celebrate Orthodox Christmas with his parish. The Yupik people were a mix of either Catholic or Russian Orthodox faith. Aata spoke of starting the longer patrols after the holidays so the faithful could celebrate as families.

The two weeks would allow for both Catholic and Orthodox holidays to be celebrated by the villagers as well as to gather more food for winter. One week would be for fishing under the river ice or the sloughs or ponds. The next week would be for hunting. They would hunt grouse, rabbits or any other game that would provide a tasty addition to the winter stores. Uncle agreed. It was decided that the next two weeks would be set aside for Christmas as well as fishing and hunting.

Sonny worked hard in the following days. In addition to the fishing and hunting, the men began to gather wood across the river for the stoves in the village. At the end of the first week, the men held a feast in the qasgiq. The Catholic priest had arrived the day before. Mass was held in the small wooden church. The entire village ate and danced. The tradition of gift giving was carried out by the entire village at the feast. Gifts of new fur mittens, mukluks, blankets and knives or pots were exchanged between the villagers. Aata received a new knife for skinning furs. Aana was happy as she was given several bolts of cloth for making qaspeqs or cloth dresses in the Yupik style. Kuukuq and Nayagaq got new mukluks. Sonny was thrilled to receive a hunting rifle from Uncle.

Aata was known as the most generous gift giver in the village. His skill in trapping gave his family an abundance of furs for making warm clothes and for trading at the store for supplies. He gave new snowshoes, dog sleds and blankets that he had made or tanned. The gifts were greatly appreciated.

Leftover food was taken home by the elders. The Yupik villagers were happy and refreshed.

At the end of the second week, another feast and dance was held. The Orthodox priest had arrived and celebrated the Christmas service. It was a more solemn occasion. Instead of gift exchanges, the faithful constructed large stars that spun like wheels. They walked through the village from cabin to cabin. They carried the spinning stars and sang ancient Christmas carols in Russian. When the carolers arrived at a cabin, they were ushered inside for a tasty meal from the family. It was a joyful celebration.

The New Year came. It was now 1943. Refreshed by the Christmas celebration, the Guards began their longer patrols. Several young unmarried men began breaking the new trails through the snow along the ancient routes. They took turns snowshoeing up and down the trail to tramp down the snow so their dog teams could move forward. They camped along the trails in the snow. It took several weeks before the trails were ready to patrol. At last the trails were open and easy to travel by dog team.

"Keep the flight path of the Lend Lease pilots safe," is what the Army had ordered. Each journey of the patrols required a week to complete. The Guards took turns patrolling in a rotation schedule. The weather was cold through the rest of the winter. Some nights were almost -50 degrees Fahrenheit. The Guards relied on their ancient Yupik traditions to survive in the harsh conditions. Their clothing was made of warm fur. Their dogs were well kept. Their knowledge of the land and how to plan for weather or other challenges was acquired from countless centuries of living on the land.

Each week, Uncle or Aata called their reports into the Army at Nome on the radio. They told the Army about the findings of each patrol. No more Japanese balloons were spotted. The trails were kept open until the spring thaw when the snow melted. Travel was difficult for a period of time until the Yukon's ice broke and drifted down river. The Guards patrolled by river boat or long hikes across the tundra as summer's long days arrived.

Chapter Nine

The Search

THE SEASONS PASSED SLOWLY IN 1943. The Guard continued to vigilantly patrol the expansive area while looking for sign of Japanese invaders. The Yupik men practiced drills with their rifles. Although less time was spent on subsistence activities, the land provided the food they needed so they did not go hungry.

Sonny was now almost as tall as Uncle. His 13th birthday arrived in February of 1943. He could keep up pace with the men. Hunting, trapping and fishing came easily to him. Aata and Aana praised him for his hard work. The elders of the village loved him dearly. Sonny often shared the fish or animals he fished or hunted with the elders of the village according to his Yupik tradition.

It seemed like a peaceful time. The year passed to 1944. However, the strain of the war hung over everyone and made life uneasy. Radio reports of battles on the Aleutian Islands showed how dangerous Japan was to Alaska. The native Aleutians were taken captive by the enemy and removed to distant Japan. Villagers on other islands, such as St. Paul Island in the Bering Sea, were evacuated to safety by the Army. They had to leave their homes and traditional way of life to wait the war out in a strange new land.

In the summer, the supplies for the trading post in Fortuna Ledge arrived by steamboat on the Yukon. The Yupik from nearby villages, including Tuckchuck, gathered on the riverbank to watch the barge arrive and unload. The workers shared news from the other villages of the river where they had stopped.

Downriver, villages of Scammon Bay and Emmonak shared how their Guards had to learn how to identify Japanese boats and submarines. They were tasked with keeping a watch for the enemy trying to enter the Yukon River and travel up it. Fortunately, no Japanese vessels had invaded the lower Yukon River.

Major Muktuk Marston returned in late summer. His plane landed on the Yukon by Fortuna Ledge. He traveled by riverboat to Tuckchuck and met with the Guards. Uncle and Aata called the men together for drills. The Major met with them for several hours. He said he was very pleased with their company. Sonny felt proud. The Major told him how amazed he was that Sonny had grown so much. The Tuckchuck Guard stood proudly on the bank of the Yukon and saluted the Major as he left on the boat to visit nearby villages.

The summer of 1944 passed to fall. Soon, the winter came with the New Year. It was the beginning of 1945.

One cold morning in early March, the Guard radio cackled in the family cabin. Everyone was startled. Aata jumped to the shelf. The Army base in Nome was calling. A plane had crashed. It had been flying from Fairbanks to Nome. The pilot had radioed for help as the plane was going down. He was not sure where he was, but he thought he was somewhere along the Yukon River. The Army called all Guards along the Yukon River to respond and join in searching for the missing plane. It was believed that the pilot had survived. They needed to find him.

Aata said the Tuckchuck Guard would start looking for the pilot immediately. As he hung up the mic, there was a knock at the cabin door. It was Uncle.

The Tuckchuck Guard was hastily called to assemble in the qasqiq. Uncle designated teams of three men each to search in their patrol area for the crashed plane. They agreed on a signal of three shots fired from their rifles if they found the plane. The search teams would cover an assigned area and meet back at an agreed upon central location a day later.

Dog teams were hitched. The dog sleds were packed with supplies. The men said goodbyes to their families and mushed their dogs out on to the trails.

Sonny drove his dog team behind Aata's on the eastern trail where they had shot down the Japanese spy balloon a few years earlier. The third man on their team was a cousin of Aata. The dogs raced over the snow as if they knew how urgent the search was.

Night came on, but the trail was lit by the moon and stars. After many hours, Aata stopped. He said they would make a fire. After eating and resting, they would continue to a lake. If they did not find the pilot or plane, they would turn around and return to the meeting spot.

Sonny struggled to keep his eyes open as he leaned over the back of his sled handle. The dogs were pulling slowly but steadily. Sonny wondered how Aata could stay awake so long. He watched his father over the hours. Aata stood straight on the sled runners. He looked from side to side on the trail to see if he could spot the plane. All the way to the frozen lake and back, Aata searched tirelessly.

It was early the next morning when Sonny and the men reached the meeting area. Some canvas tents had been set up. Inside the tents, wood stoves warmed the men as they returned from the trails. Dogs were staked in a large open area, far apart to keep them from fighting. After eating a tasty meal, the dogs curled up and rested. The men cooked and ate before lying wearily in their warm caribou blankets on the floor of the tents.

After a short hour of much needed sleep, Sonny was awakened by the loud chorus of dogs barking. A dog team had arrived from Fortuna Ledge. The Guard Captain from upriver had come to share the news. The Guard company from Ruby, an Athabaskan village many miles up the Yukon, had found the pilot. He was brought safely by dog team to the village. A plane with skis landed on the runway that had been cleared of snow on the Yukon in front of Ruby. The injured pilot was taken to the hospital in Fairbanks.

Major Marston had gotten on the radio and thanked all the brave men of the Guard. He praised the villagers along the Yukon River for their search efforts. He said they helped save the life of a much needed pilot.

The Tuckchuck men cheered the news. Even though they were all still very tired, they decided to break the camp and return home to their village.

The rest of the winter passed quietly. Spring thaw brought the crash and boom of the Yukon River ice breaking. When the icebergs reached the Bering Sea, the Yukon quieted and summer arrived. The family returned to fish camp.

Chapter Ten

VICTORY
1945

IT WAS AUGUST 6, 1945. SONNY, frowned. He could feel a change coming. He studied the camp around him carefully. Sonny couldn't figure out what was making him feel uneasy and excited at the same time. He paused and studied the sky. It was his 15th summer. He stood on the bank of Kuigpak, the Yukon River, in Western Alaska.

Sonny looked around. Aata and Uncle were mending nets on the top of the river bank. Kuukuq was playing with a small bow and arrows that Aata had made for him to hunt small animals such as grouse and rabbits. Nayagaq was in the tent with Aana. The radio on the wooden table in the tent was softly playing music. They were mixing bannock bread to eat with the evening meal of fish. Around the fish camp, the dogs were staked and slept in the warm sunny afternoon. The smoke house was full of silver salmon which ran in the Yukon in the fall. Blue wisps of smoke lazily lifted from the fire in the yard and in the smokehouse.

Then a man's voice came on the radio. He was speaking about Japan. Aana stepped to the tent opening and called Aata. Aata and Uncle dropped the nets and came to listen, with Sonny and Kuukuq following.

"Today, the United States has dropped the first atomic bomb on Hiroshima, Japan. Our brave men flew in the Enola Gay from the Mariana Islands for six hours to Japan. The bomb, codenamed Little Boy, was dropped on the manufacturing city of Hiroshima. The first atomic bomb was a success. The reports of damage are still coming in."

After dinner, Aata and Uncle sat at the fire and discussed the radio report. Uncle decided to radio the Army in Nome to find out what was going on. He had brought the radio to fish camp and went in the tent to call.

The Army confirmed the bombing of Hiroshima. The soldier hoped that Japan would soon surrender. It would be the end of the war. It would be a victory for the United States.

Aata and Uncle rejoined their discussions at the fire. They talked about how Germany had surrendered in May. The Soviets had bombed the Germans using the planes that had been flown from Alaska.

Sonny listened. He began to cough. Aata told him to move away from the smoke from the fire. Later that night, as Sonny lay awake in the tent, he tried not to cough and keep his family awake. He had overheard Aana whisper to Aata. She was worried about Sonny's cough. Aata had noticed the coughing too. He told Aana that he would take Sonny to the doctor in Fortuna Ledge if the coughing continued after they left fish camp.

The radio reported more news about the war two days later. The voice announced that the Soviets had declared war on Japan. The Soviet Army began invading a place called Manchuria in China. The man on the radio wondered why Japan did not surrender but kept on fighting.

The next day, the news came over the radio that the United

States had dropped another atomic bomb on the Japanese city of Nagasaki. This bomb was codenamed Fat Man and it was a bigger bomb than Little Boy. Many Japanese died from the atomic bombs.

Six days later, on August 15th, 1945, the Emperor of Japan surrendered. The war was over! The Guard gathered in Tuckchuck to share the news. Major Marston called on the radio and thanked the men for helping win the victory in the war. He told them that he was proud of all the "Eskimo scouts." They had used their experience and knowledge of living off the land to be the eyes and ears of the United States Army. The men of Tuckchuck had done their part to protect the freedom of the great nation of the United States. Governor Gruening also spoke and thanked all the brave men and women from all across Alaska who came together without pay or compensation to be ready to fight for their country.

The Yupik of Tuckchuck celebrated with a feast in the village. They danced and sang in Yupik tradition. The war was over.

Chapter Eleven

New Beginnings
1946

While reminiscing at his sister's fish camp in August of 1978, Sonny smiled as he remembered when he had shot the bear at fish camp. He savored the memory a moment. Shooting the bear had taken the very depth of his bravery and quick action. The success had given him courage. He had needed it. Sonny's thoughts wandered back to another time when he needed that courage. The courage he was not to face a bear but a different danger. It was a danger from within his own body.

The tuberculosis that Sonny had contracted by the end of 1945 had lingered and worsened. He began to cough up blood. Uncle warned Aata that the coughing was serious and urged him to take Sonny to the doctor before the younger children got sick. Several Yupik elders in Tuckchuck and nearby villages had died from the cough.

Sonny lost weight and felt weak all the time. He could not go with Aata to hunt and fish. He lay in bed all day and moaned softly in pain. The coughing hurt his lungs and the spasms strained the muscles of his midsection.

The first time Sonny saw a doctor for his tuberculosis, he had to leave Tuckchuck to travel to Bethel. He was only sixteen. He had never been so far from home in his life. Sonny's English was broken. His heart pounded in his chest. He tried to be brave. He was determined to go to the hospital to get better and come home to work hard at hunting and trapping like a true Yupik man. Sonny said goodbye to Aana and Aata and tried not to look at their worried faces.

A plane landed at Fortuna Ledge to fly Sonny to Bethel. There was a hospital in Bethel. The hospital was noisy and confusing. The doctor listened to Sonny's chest grimly. The doctor ordered Sonny to be placed in a bed on a ward. Sonny missed his village and the beautiful sound of Yupik spoken there as he lay in the bed and listened to the unfamiliar English spoken around him.

Sonny winced at the memory. Sonny returned to the reflection in his mind and recalled how his youthful body ached from inactivity. His chest burned with the infection. He struggled for breath. The coughing hurt. It was the desire to go home to his parents that kept him fighting to get well.

Sonny fought. After six months, he flew home.

Aata was grateful for Sonny's return. His father needed the help with the hard work of subsistence food gathering. Aana fussed over him. She said Sonny was too skinny. She fed him the choicest bits of fatty meats and fish. Aana made agutak, the Eskimo ice cream of lard, berries and white fish combined, often and served her son large portions.

After World War II had ended, accounts of the brave deeds of the Native men and women across Alaska spread among the Yupik villages. Many young Native men had stayed enlisted in the Army or joined other branches of the United States military. Young men left Tuckchuck and Fortuna Ledge to keep serving their country in the armed forces. Sonny dreamed of following them when he turned nineteen. He wanted to find an outlet for his bravery and cunning. It was a bitter truth when the doctor in Bethel told him that the tuberculosis would prevent him from any more military service. The time for his dream was lost.

Years passed. Sonny worked hard. His accomplishments in hunting, trapping and fishing were respected. He gained weight back and grew lean muscle. Things seemed to come to Sonny easily. Shooting, setting fishing nets or traps resulted in successful harvesting. He spent most of his time at the qasgiq now. He carved ivory with the other men into small figures to sell. He made snowshoes and dogsleds. Sonny helped the men of the village with Yuuraq or dancing and ceremonies and celebrations.

He had not attended school past the third grade. He encouraged Nayagaq and Kuukuq to study hard. After spending months in the hospital in Bethel, he knew they needed to learn more of the white man's ways to do well in life. The next two years were busy and blissful. Sonny grew and thrived. The passage of time put the war further and further behind the men of the Yukon.

Uncle began to tease Sonny about getting a wife and starting his own family. Sonny blushed. Then, one day, in exasperation, Sonny burst out in reply to his uncle's teasing, "Every woman I know is my relative!"

Uncle was silent a long time. Then, he patted Sonny's arm reassuringly, "You will find a wife. You are a nukalpiaq! Any woman would be proud to be your wife! You will provide everything she needs. Someday, you will meet a woman who is not your relative and you will know that she is the one for you!"

Uncle's words sparked a longing in Sonny's heart. As the year passed and he turned twenty, the long months took a heavy toll on the spark. It began to sputter out and hope dwindled. Sonny was coughing up blood again. The tuberculosis was back. Once again, Sonny left for Bethel. Once again, he struggled not to look at his parent's devastated faces.

Aana hugged him tight, "I won't see you again for a long time, Sonny!" Her body convulsed in sobs.

Taken aback, Aata and Sonny tried to assure her that in few months Aana would hug her son again. Aana shook her head. "I don't mean that. Sonny, you will find a life out there. When you get better and leave the hospital this time, you will find a life out there."

Sonny thought about Aana's words all the plane ride to Bethel. The words did not make sense. He was too tired to figure it out. He wearily returned to the bed in the tuberculosis ward.

The next morning, Sonny awoke as a nurse gently shook him. He opened his eyes. She was blond and her eyes were of a pale blue that he could not quit staring at. Her white cap and crisp dress uniform shone like an angel. She smiled kindly. Sonny's heart raced.

The months passed quickly for Sonny. He recovered steadily under the nurse's care. Then, he was discharged from the hospital. Sonny walked out into the crisp Bethel air. He felt alive again. He felt free.

Sonny walked around Bethel that day, looking for work. A man at the store told him that canneries in Dillingham were hiring for salmon processing workers. Sonny found the cannery man and signed up.

He had brought some of his ivory carvings with him to finish while he was in the hospital. He showed them to the store owner. The shop keeper was impressed and bought all of the carvings at a good price. Sonny bought some new clothes and a room for a week until he would leave to work as a fish processor. He combed his hair and decided to attend a movie.

As Sonny walked into the movie theater, it took a minute for his eyes to adjust. He stared. There was the blond nurse! His heart thudded as he took a chair on the end of the row near where she sat. He glanced over. She had not seen him.

Sonny took a deep breath. He recalled his uncle's words, "Any woman would be proud to be your wife!" He moved a seat nearer to her. As the movie played across the screen, Sonny waited a minute or two before moving a seat closer to the nurse. Finally, he was next to her. She looked up at him. She smiled prettily. He put his arm around her shoulders.

Sonny began dating the nurse. They fell in deep love, holding hands while taking long walks together. The nurse did not seem to mind Sonny's broken English. Sonny loved to gaze into her blue eyes. He thought of the ancient legend of the crane that the elder of Tuckchuck had taught him when he was young. He considered that Crane was very intelligent for choosing blueberries to replace its eyes. He was sure that he could build a good life with such an intelligent woman whose eyes were a captivating blue.

As time went by, Sonny found the courage to ask a bold question of the nurse. Sonny asked her if she would be Nuliaq, his nuliaq, meaning his wife. She nodded.

Nuliaq and Sonny were married by the Catholic priest several months later. Nuliaq worked at the hospital while Sonny worked the salmon season in Dillingham. They rejoined in Bethel that fall with money saved up. Nuliaq asked Sonny if he wanted to live in Kodiak where she had first arrived in Alaska to work as a nurse.

Sonny realized what Aana had meant when she had tearfully told him that he would move away from his Yupik village and not return. He wondered how Aana had known that her son would meet a non-Yupik woman. Now, he finally understood. Aana had let him know that she understood. In a way, Aana had given her approval of Sonny's choice to leave his Yupik world behind. He felt free and excited. New experiences and a new country awaited him in Kodiak. He was ready for daring and adventure!

THIRTY-SIX YEARS LATER, SONNY SAT ON the bench outside the tent at fish camp and tried to recall the feeling of excitement he had when he was first married. He couldn't. It seemed so long ago.

He thought about his daughter. Sonny spent a moment wondering if she had felt excitement when she left home for boarding school. He sighed and returned to his memories.

Chapter Twelve

Major Change
1960

Sonny chuckled softly as he returned to the present moment. He poured another cup of coffee as quietly as he could. The sun was still below the far hills beyond the banks of the Yukon and the fish camp lay in a gray stillness. The land was still and silent. Sonny returned to his reminiscing. The same excitement he had felt as the boy waiting for the plane was the same excitement he had experienced when he had taken the plane with his new wife from Dillingham to Kodiak.

Sonny gave his complete devotion to his marriage with the blond nurse. He finished working many grueling hours at the fish processing plant to save enough for the move to Kodiak. The couple now had plane tickets and a down payment to rent a house on the largest island in Alaska.

When they landed in Kodiak, a friend of Nuliaq met them at the airport with a car. They drove to a house where the landlord waited. He rented to them immediately. The next day, Nuliaq went to the hospital and came home with a job.

Sonny felt out of sorts. He did not know anyone and he was out of work. As a husband, he felt he should be working instead of Nuliaq. Nuliaq urged him to talk to some of her former acquaintances the next day. Her friend was a fellow nurse who was married to an Alutiiq man. The Alutiiq man guided hunts for Kodiak bears in the spring. The bear hunting guide also had a commercial fishing vessel and needed a crew for the salmon season. Sonny felt hopeful. He knew how to hunt and how to handle nets for salmon.

The next day was Saturday. Sonny and Nuliaq went downtown Kodiak. Nuliaq had owned a Jeep when she had previously lived in Kodiak. She wanted to buy another one. After they bought the Jeep, they drove to her friend's house so Sonny could ask the guide for work.

The guide greeted Sonny warmly. Sonny immediately felt he would get along well with his new friend. They shared bear hunting stories. The guide explained that there was a short season for hunting bear in the fall. He invited Sonny to start work for him in the next month, which was November. They agreed to meet again on Monday at the Kodiak boat harbor. The guide wanted to show Sonny his commercial fishing vessel.

On Monday, Sonny kissed his wife as she left to work at the hospital. He cleaned the kitchen and walked downtown to the boat harbor. It was raining. The visibility was shortened to a dull fog that hung over the town. He wished it was clear so he could study the lay of the land as he walked. He had not had time to learn about the land that surrounded Kodiak. He knew that Pillar Mountain rose above the town and harbor. Nuliaq had said the small island across from the harbor was Woody Island.

Sonny began to whistle. His health had been getting better. He looked forward to working again. Hard work was his anchor in life as a man. He felt the excitement of new adventure rise inside. New land. New friends. New life.

Sonny found the harbor and the guide. The guide showed him around his boat proudly. The vessel was a thirty-two foot gill netter. There was a berth below for sleeping and a tiny kitchen for meals to be eaten while the commercial fishing crew was at work on the water. The guide made a pot of coffee and the two men sat in the wheelhouse talking.

The guide shared that the Kodiak bears are the largest in Alaska and the United States. He explained that his clients were wealthy men from cities across the Lower 48, such as New York and Texas. He chuckled as he told Sonny that the men started the hunt bravely and full of arrogance. When the massive 10 foot tall bears that weighed some 1,500 pounds approached the hunting party, the true measure of the men's courage or lack of courage became apparent. Some men bravely raised their rifles and shot the bears accurately. When the same men posed with the bear, they became shaken with shock while realizing the enormous size of the animal they had killed. Other men panicked at the first sight of the size of the bears, cowered and never took the shot. Occasionally, but not often, the bears charged when they were wounded by a poor shot. The lives of all the men in the hunting party depended on the back up guide to shoot the charging bear and stop it from harming anyone.

The guide showed Sonny the heavy rifle that he would be carrying as back up guide. It was an elephant gun or a .500 Nitro Express. It was heavy and had a sling to carry on the long hikes up the mountain slopes where the bears were hunted.

The guide told Sonny that he would find the clothes and gear he needed for the hunt they would guide when the hunting party went out the next month at the store downtown. He offered to hire Sonny immediately to help him with net repairs and other chores he needed to do before the onset of winter. Sonny shook his hand and agreed to start the next day.

Sonny walked home. It had stopped raining but the clouds still hung low over the island. He hummed as he walked. Nuliaq was home and already cooking dinner. As they ate, Sonny told her about his new job and she shared what her day of nursing had been like. Sonny smiled as he listened and looked into her blue eyes. He felt good in his heart.

The next day dawned clear and sunny. The air was crisp as Sonny walked to the boat harbor. The guide met him at the gangway. They boarded the boat and found the gill nets on deck. The guide left again as Sonny began the tedious difficult job of checking each net and repairing them where they needed repairing. At first, Sonny's fingers hurt from so little use. As the day passed, Sonny became too engrossed in his diligent work to mind his discomfort. As his Yupik father and uncle had taught him to work hard with a deep concentration and keenness of accuracy, he repaired the nets.

The month went by quickly. Sonny walked down the steep hill from his house every morning and back home in the evening. The soreness in his hands, back and legs gradually gave way to strong muscles. The guide was impressed with Sonny's diligent work ethic. The guide began to stand by Sonny to talk with him as he worked. Sonny enjoyed the company. Soon, the two men were laughing heartily over each other's anecdotes.

After a time, the guide reviewed all the details of guiding the scheduled Kodiak bear hunt. He placed a map on the galley table of the fishing vessel. They found the location of the guide's bear camp. It was a half day's travel by the vessel. They made a plan to visit the camp a week before the hunters arrived to stock supplies and set everything up.

AT THE FISH CAMP, THE BENCH creaked a little as Sonny shifted and drew back to his present moment. The sides of his mouth curled slightly into a smile as he recalled the early days of his marriage in Kodiak. Everything was so new and exciting. He drew a deep breath, and his mind went back to his time in Kodiak.

Chapter Thirteen

READINESS
1960

SONNY CONTINUED REMINISCING AS HE REFLECTED on his first job with the guide on the Kodiak bear hunt.

The guide had begun earnest preparations for the November bear hunt. He introduced Sonny to the third member of the party, the camp cook. The cook was a quiet dark man from the Alutiiq village of Port Lyons on Kodiak Island. Like Sonny, his first language was his native tongue. The cook was reticent, focused and spoke little. He had been a backup gun man for the guide for years but wanted to stay in the camp to cook instead of going hiking in the mountains on hunts. He proved himself to be much more than a cook. The man was short but strong. He carried the heavy loads of supplies onto the boat with ease. He arranged the boxes neatly and securely.

The men set sail for the hunting camp one sunny morning in early November. They planned to spend several nights at the camp to prepare it for the clients. The guide showed Sonny how to pilot the vessel. He pointed out their course on the navigational charts. He quickly shared how to read the ship's compass and follow the charts. The guide told Sonny to take the helm as he went below to nap on the bunk.

Sonny's brow furrowed as he concentrated on his task. To his relief, the cook stood at his elbow. The cook talked him through piloting the boat along the voyage. The two men began to share stories as was the custom of native people. The Alutiiq and Yupik had a lot in common.

The cook told Sonny countless stories of bear hunting done by his own people. He shared native lore passed on from many generations of Alutiiq. He talked about what he learned from the hunting he had done with the guide and his Lower 48 clients.

Sonny recounted to the cook the story of his own experience when he was 12 years old at fish camp on the Yukon with his family and how he had shot the charging bear. The cook nodded solemnly after listening to Sonny's story. He patted Sonny's arm and told him that it was good that he had that success as a bear hunter. He warned Sonny that he would need it for the formidable Kodiak bear. The cook continued sharing his knowledge. He told Sonny as much as he could about the island, the bears and the ways of the Alutiiq. Sonny studied him as he spoke. The cook was staring straight ahead as he talked as if he were reading the waters. Sonny felt he had a good friend in the cook.

The vessel handled very differently on the ocean water than how Sonny's family skiff had cut through the river waters on the Yukon. The tides and currents of the Pacific Ocean around Kodiak Island were a new challenge for Sonny. He concentrated as Aata had taught him to concentrate when faced with new challenges. The Yupik tradition of learning new skills empowered Sonny. He was far from his home on the Yukon, but he felt he could do well on Kodiak Island.

The cook teased Sonny about seasickness. Sonny admitted he felt slightly queasy when the vessel first left Kodiak harbor but at the present he did not notice any nausea. The cook laughed, gently hit Sonny's arm and said something in his language. Sonny could see by the look in the cook's eyes that he admired Sonny's companionship.

The men arrived at the hunting camp in the early afternoon. As they anchored the larger vessel offshore in the deeper water, they noticed a large brown bear walking the shore near the camp. As they filled the skiff with supplies, they kept an eye on the bear. They were relieved when it walked up the bank. It continued up the slopes until it disappeared over a ridge high above the camp.

The camp was comprised of a wooden cabin bunkhouse, a sturdy kitchen and a larger shed. Each building was solidly fortified against any marauding bears. A firepit lay in the middle of the yard with wooden benches around it. The brush around the buildings had been cleared. Over the summer, tall shrubs called devil's club had grown over the yard and along the trail from the beach. The autumn frosts had killed the shrubs and they lay shriveled and flat. The men were relieved that the devil's club was flattened so they could clearly see whether bears were near the camp.

The guide began opening the buildings and storing the supplies. The cook and Sonny made several trips in the skiff back to the boat for the rest of the supplies. The men worked hard until dusk. The cook served a delicious dinner. The men built up the fire in the yard and sat around it contentedly. Sonny spoke of his wish for a steam bath. He shared how Yupik men bathed in the kashim by building a fire to heat up rocks. The men splashed water over the rocks for steam. The clouds of steam caused the men to sweat. After a time, they went outside and poured cold water over their bodies. The Alutiiq agreed. He said his village had the same customs. The guide laughed. He pointed to some buckets in the shed. The men could splash cold water from a nearby stream to clean up.

The cook hauled several pails of water and the men washed their faces and hands before retiring to the bunkhouse for the night. The heavy wooden door was shut tight with a wooden bar across it. Each man had a loaded rifle within quick reach near his bunk. Sonny sank into his warm sleeping bag. He said a quick prayer for Nuliaq to be safe and not feel too lonely for him that night. He immediately fell into a deep slumber.

Sonny woke. He stared into the inky blackness of the interior of the bunkhouse. He listened. He could hear the waves on the bank above the beach. He surmised that the tide was high. Suddenly, there was a strange sound! That is what must have awakened him. He lifted himself up on his elbow to listen intently.

The cook whispered in the dark. It was a sea lion on the shores. Sonny lay back down. He did not waken until morning.

The cook rose first and made strong coffee. The men gratefully drank the coffee black and began the arduous work of preparing the camp for the hunt. It took them all morning to haul supplies, unpack and get the bunkhouse ready for guests.

As the cook began arranging the kitchen and preparations for the evening meal, the guide told Sonny to join him. The guide packed a spotting scope on a tripod and his bear gun. He handed Sonny a pair of high-powered binoculars. Sonny slipped the binoculars around his neck and adjusted his rifle sling over his shoulder. The rifle was cumbersome.

The guide led the way along a trail that ran across the creek. The trail swung around the bottom of a knoll before zigzagging up the base of the nearest mountain. The men hiked for an hour. The climb was intensely strenuous. The weight of the burdensome rifle caused the sling to dig into Sonny's shoulder.

The guide breathed heavily as he made his way up the trail. Sonny was happy that walking up a steep slope had become easy for him when he walked to and from house to his work the previous weeks.

At last, the guide reached an outcropping. He left the trail and went towards a boulder that jutted out of the mountain. Sonny followed. As the men stood on the rock, the vista that lay before them caused them to pause in wonder as they caught their breath.

The guide sat down and got his spotting scope set up on the tripod. He pointed to the valley and slopes beyond their vantage point. Sonny lifted his binoculars. He scanned the area carefully. On a far side of a hillock over a creek that ran down the mountain slope was a line of brush. The brush consisted of thick alders whose branches were now bare of leaves.

Sonny looked over the brush again. A giant brown figure rose out of the creek and climbed through the alder brush to a meadow on the slope. It was a bear! Sonny tapped the guide's arm and pointed. The guide turned his scope toward where Sonny gestured. He whispered excitedly, "Nice! That's a big bear!" He watched the Kodiak bear a moment before packing his scope away. "The clients will like that one! Good job, Sonny! Way to find the bear right away. You are the perfect man for this job!"

The men hiked silently on their return. Going downhill was much easier and they expeditiously made their way back to camp. The aroma of bread baking made their stomachs growl. The cook was still finishing a stew to go with the rolls.

While waiting patiently for their dinner, the guide and Sonny sat in the yard. The guide did not want to light the fire. He explained that he did not want to drive the big bear they had seen further away by burning a yard fire. He planned to leave early the next morning. The clients would arrive by the end of the week and they would be returning immediately to begin the hunt after they landed in Kodiak.

The guide told Sonny that there was a gravel pit outside of the city of Kodiak. He wanted to take Sonny there and practice target shooting with the rifles. It was a matter of life and death that Sonny be familiar and ready with his rifle. Sonny agreed. The guide said he did not want to practice with the rifles at the camp. The gunshots would scare the bears away into the mountains.

The cook came outside and told the two men that the stew was ready. He wiped his hands on his apron and turned to Sonny. He asked Sonny whether he liked the rifle he was packing. Sonny admitted that it was heavy. The heavy rifle made hiking up steep slopes difficult.

The cook nodded. He told Sonny that he had another rifle that was powerful but lighter. It was a .375 H and H. He explained that the rifle had been given to him but he didn't need it. He planned to stick to cooking and staying in the camp during the hunt. The cook shared that he occasionally liked to go hunting for the small Sitka black tail deer. However, his grandsons did most of the hunting now and he was content to trade the job of backup hunter for being the cook in the camp. He told Sonny that if he liked the gun, he could buy it from him in payments. Sonny agreed.

That night, Sonny slept soundly. The sea lions did not waken him at all. It was still dark when the men rose. They drank their coffee in silence. Afterwards, the men shut the doors of the camp buildings tightly so the bears could not break in and eat the supplies. It was just getting light when the three men alighted the skiff and rowed to the boat. The trip back to Kodiak was calm and swift.

The next morning, Sonny walked to work. He headed to the harbor. The guide was waiting for him. He pointed to the rifles leaning in the middle of the front seat. The guide had stopped by the cook's house and picked up the new rifle for Sonny to practice with. The guide placed several boxes of ammunition on the seat and told Sonny to get in. They got in the guide's truck and drove from the city.

The guide pulled into the gravel pit. On the far end of the open pit was a jumble of targets that were full of bullet holes. The men took the rifles out and began shooting. Sonny found that the .500 Nitro Express had a powerful kick when he pulled the trigger. The rifle butt bruised his shoulder. He practiced shooting the big gun. He threw it up and shot. He stepped to the side and quickly shot. After he felt he had mastered the Nitro, Sonny picked up the .375 H and H. He immediately liked the feel of the new rifle. He found he was faster with it and more accurate. Sonny decided to buy the new rifle from the cook.

The guide was pleased with Sonny's rifle marksmanship. As he drove Sonny back to Kodiak, he talked the entire way about hunts from the years past. Sonny listened carefully. He knew well how dangerous the bears were.

SONNY BREATHED DEEPLY AS HE SAT on the bench at fish camp. The Kodiak bear hunts were exciting. He was glad he practiced. He had learned that practice was important many years before in the Guard back in Tuckchuck. He recalled the military drills he practiced with his father.

Chapter Fourteen

The Charge
1960

Sonny drew his thoughts back to the present. He was mildly surprised that the sun had not risen yet at fish camp. In the tent, his sister and her children still slept soundly. Nothing seemed to stir. It seemed as if time had frozen. He thought it was because he needed to reminisce. He drifted back into memory. The drills and practice had helped him when he needed it the most. The bear hunt on Kodiak Island was when Sonny had needed to use his practiced skills.

The weather in Kodiak was mercifully clear. The November days were warmer than usual. The guide was happy. His hunting guests were arriving at the airport that morning. The guest had flown from Seattle to Anchorage where they spent the night. Then, they flew to Kodiak the next morning.

The cook and Sonny waited on the boat. They went over everything one more time to make sure all was in order. Sonny thanked the cook for the new rifle. The cook nodded and replied that he had been sure Sonny would like it. He added that the rifle had a lot of power just like the Nitro but it was easier for Sonny to carry.

The two men finished checking the gear over and stood waiting on the deck for the guide to arrive with the two clients. Sonny asked the cook if he had ever met the men before on a previous hunt. The cook shook his head. All the cook knew was that the two men were very rich. One was an oil company man from Texas and the other man was his friend from California. When Sonny heard this, he began to wonder if the men knew how to shoot and hunt. He frowned as he remembered the steep trail that the guide took him on at the camp. He asked himself what would be expected of him if the men could not hike.

The cook was watching Sonny's face and laughed. The Alutiiq began to tell stories about past seasons and the variety of hunters he and the guide had taken bear hunting. There was one client who was a famous actor from Hollywood. The actor arrived drunk and drank the entire hunt. The celebrity stayed in camp. There was no bear hunting. There was a companion with the man. He apparently was the actor's agent. The agent made the guide and the cook swear to secrecy over the so-called hunt. The actor left on the appointed day at the end of the guided bear hunt with a horrible hangover. The agent gave the guide a large sum of money as a tip.

The cook shared some more stories as the men waited. He finished when they saw the guide arriving at the harbor with two men. "Just make sure no one gets hurt," the cook said as he patted Sonny's back. Sonny looked at the cook. The cook winked back. Sonny chuckled. It seemed the cook was warning him that the hunters were not very skilled.

The guide arrived at the boat. He introduced the clients to Sonny and the cook. The two men looked at Sonny and the cook and looked away. It was as if they dismissed the two Native men. Sonny set to work loading the men's backpacks onto the boat.

The Texan had a large rifle case in his gear. He yelled at Sonny to be careful with it before yanking it from his hands. The Texan patted the gun case and told the guide that he had just bought a very expensive scope for the rifle. He had the scope mounted and sighted in at the gun shop in Texas where he bought it. The Texan loudly declared he was ready for the bears.

The two clients ignored Sonny and the cook the entire way to the camp. Sonny heard the man from California murmur something about Natives but he could not make out the words. Sonny began to feel uncomfortable. He looked at the cook as he was sitting in a corner and staring at the floor. The guide chatted busily with the clients as he piloted the boat across the waters.

The hunting party reached the camp in the late afternoon. A slight wind had arisen. The leafless alders along the shore whistled softly as the men landed in the skiff. Sonny and the cook set to work immediately as the guide showed the guests around.

The cook delivered a delicious dinner after a few hours. As Sonny and the cook cleaned up the dishes, the guide and his clients sat in the bunkhouse. They sipped whiskey and talked over the plans for the next day.

Sonny slept deeply again that night. The cook woke him before all the others. Sonny helped him make coffee and breakfast. The guide and all the men ate quickly. There was an air of anticipation over the camp for the day's bear hunt.

The cook stayed in camp while Sonny and the guide left with the hunters. They crossed the creek and began up the hill. The Texan began to breathe heavily as he strained up the steep trail. The Californian began to lag. Sonny was told to carry the California's rifle until they got to the rock overlook. It took the hunting party a long time to reach the rock outcropping. The sun was now high in the sky.

The Texan and the Californian paused gasping for air, as the guide waited for them to join him on the rock to look for bears on the slopes beyond. Sonny helped them take their packs off and dig out their canteens. He gingerly leaned their rifles up against the rock. He was grateful that the two men were too winded to yell at him to be careful.

The guide had set his spotting scope on the tripod to look for bears. As the hunters caught their second wind and settled on the flat rock area, the guide whispered instructions on how they were going to proceed.

As the guide spoke, Sonny pulled out his binoculars and began scanning the ravine where he had seen the bear the week before. There was nothing in sight. Sonny lowered his binoculars and waited for the guide to finish whispering. It was disappointing that the bear had left the area. It was going to be difficult to hike further with the two men from the Lower 48.

Then there was a loud grunt and the cracking of brush! Sonny instinctively removed his sling and the rifle from his shoulder without pausing to think. The guide held up his hand to silence the others. The party looked in the direction of the sounds. Some 20 yards away was the huge bear!

The bear was on the same elevation of the slope as the hunting party. It had winded them and was moving up the mountain side a few feet before stopping to sniff the air.

The Texan leapt up and grabbed his rifle. He threw it up to his shoulder and aimed before the guide or anyone else could react. Bam! The shot rang out deafeningly loud. The Californian gave a little cry as he rolled to his side on the ground.

Everything happened in an instant. The bear roared as the bullet struck it in the front shoulder, grazing the massive muscle. It charged across the slope. The patches of alder brush did nothing to slow the massive beast's charge.

The guide had set his rifle down and was frozen for the moment. He had not expected his client to shoot before he told him to.

The Texan gave a whimper as he slid his rifle bolt. The spent bullet popped out on the ground. Then, the next bullet spit out on the ground. Then, another bullet flew out. The Texan was panicking and unloading his rifle bullet by bullet. The bear was closing in on 20 feet now!

Sonny aimed his rifle and pulled the trigger. The bear's head went down. The bear hit the ground and slid. It was now five feet away. Sonny waited a second. By now, the guide had his rifle and he shot the bear to make sure it was dead.

It was.

The guide burst out. "Sonny, you saved us!" He turned to his clients. They were shaking. Dark patches in their pants revealed that they had wet themselves. The pair were frozen in stunned silence.

The guide was pleased. The bear was one of the biggest he had ever gotten for his hunters. He joked that it was a "Texas-sized bear for a Texan."

The Texan was silent. He sullenly retrieved the cartridges he had cocked out of his rifle and sat down. Finally, he spoke and in a strained voice, he demanded to go back to camp NOW.

The guide took the men back to camp. Sonny stayed to begin dressing the bear. After an hour of hard skinning, he looked up at a sound. It was the cook making his way up the steep trail. The cook admired the bear. He wanted to hear how the hunt had gone. Sonny told him. The cook laughed. He laughed so hard he had to sit down.

Sonny and the cook spent the rest of the day packing the bear down to the camp. It was getting dark when they finished their last load. The guide had cooked a meal and they ate.

The Californian did not want to hunt a bear for himself. He insisted on leaving the next day. The night passed in a quiet somber mood. Sonny had to avoid looking at the cook. Every time the cook caught Sonny's eye, he smiled broadly. It made Sonny want to break out into laughter. But, he knew that laughing would be the end of his job if the rich clients thought he was mocking them.

The guests woke up before daylight. They wanted coffee and to get going. The guide took them in the skiff to the boat first. Then, Sonny and the cook helped break down the camp and load supplies back onto the boat.

The Texan had posed for a picture with the bear hide before he left the camp. He did not smile. He looked broken. No one said anything.

That was the only bear hunt that fall. It was Sonny's first. After the guide returned to Kodiak safely with his clients and saw them off safely on the plane, he began to brag all around town about Sonny's saving shot. The people of Kodiak now recognized Sonny about town. They stopped and offered him a ride if they drove past while he was walking. Job offers came pouring in from boat captains and other guides.

The recognition Sonny appreciated most was from his wife. Her blue eyes sparkled when she looked at him. He had made her proud.

Sonny and Nuliaq enjoyed long drives in her jeep exploring Kodiak. She taught him how to drive the standard transmission and he quickly excelled in driving. She held parties at their house when she was off duty from the hospital. Life was full of excitement during those years.

One day, Nuliaq came to Sonny and wrapped her arms around him. She whispered that she wanted to start a family to share their love and home with. Sonny was overjoyed with the news. He had steady work year-round now. He worked on a crabbing vessel in the winter. He helped the guide with spring bear hunts. He was first mate on the commercial salmon fishing boat in the summer. Then, he was back up gun a second time in the year for the short autumn season of guided bear hunts. Life was good.

SONNY REFLECTED ON HIS HAPPY YEARS with Nuliaq on Kodiak. His years as a Guard in Tuckchuck that had given him the skills to work and succeed in Kodiak. He thought back on those years of being an Alaska Territorial Guard.

THE WAVE

Chapter Fifteen

THE WAVE
1964

SONNY'S THOUGHTS RETURNED TO THE PRESENT as he sat on the bench at fish camp along the Yukon. He gave a soft sigh as his memories of Kodiak came to mind again.

SONNY HAD DEDICATED HIMSELF TO BE the best husband he could be after the November bear hunt. He liked the way Nuliaq looked at him now, and began to feel comfortable in Kodiak. Working hard for long hours before enjoying parties and outdoor activities with Nuliaq during his time off was fun. It was different from his traditional Yupik childhood, but he felt a thrill of excitement as he experienced new and strange adventures.

Sonny found that whatever he put his mind to he excelled at. In addition to the fishing and guiding, he learned to repair the Jeep. His mechanical skills progressed to an expert level, and he enjoyed it when his wife's friends consulted him for help on their cars. He learned carpentry and woodworking. He like to build things out of wood. Sonny also carved ivory. He patiently carved a man, a dogsled and a dog team out of ivory when stormy days prevented him from working outside.

Once while on a commercial fishing opening for red salmon, the vessel was loaded with red salmon. As the men brought the catch to the fish processor, Sonny recognized a Yupik man working at the processor. It was his cousin from Fortuna Ledge. The cousin greeted him in Yupik. It felt good to talk in Yupik again, so Sonny readily replied.

The cousin was working in the fish processing plant for the red salmon season which lasted only a few more weeks. He was going to take his pay for the season and go back to Fortuna Ledge to build a cabin for his wife who was expecting their first child and waiting for him to return. He told Sonny all the news from Tuckchuck and Fortuna Ledge.

Sonny felt a pang of homesickness. The news from home touched his heart. His father was slowing down and his mother was worried about Aata's health. Sonny's sister was grown up. She was planning to get married in the coming year. His younger brother was starting to run with the young boys of the village. Kuukuq was not the hunter, trapper and dog team driver that Sonny was. Kuukuq wanted to move to Bethel and live a different life from the traditional village life.

When Sonny told Nuliaq that he had visited with his cousin, she was delighted. She put together a box of gifts for his family and insisted that he give it to his cousin to bring back to Tuckchuck. She wrote letters to his parents, sister and brother and slipped a little money in the envelopes. Sonny gave the gifts to his cousin. The cousin took everything back to Tuckchuck with him. A few weeks later, a letter arrived from Nayagaq. It was the beginning of an exchange of correspondence between Sonny's wife and his sister through the years. Nuliaq filled boxes with yarn, cloth for sewing and warm clothes each Christmas and sent them to Sonny's sister. She sent Nayagaq pictures and more money when she could. It pleased Sonny that Nuliaq was so kind to his family.

In 1960, Sonny's wife woke one morning sick. She told him she had to take some time off of work because she felt nauseated. Sonny had to work at the dock during the day. He was needed to unload crabbing boats. When he returned home late that night, he was exhausted. He had taken the Jeep to work, but it had rained and the Jeep slid in the mud on the way up the steep road to his house. He wearily went inside the kitchen and ate his supper cold before stumbling off to bed.

Sonny's wife was lying in bed and awakened when he entered. He mumbled an apology for waking her. She sat up, turned on the light and turned her blue eyes at him as if she was wide awake. He hesitated, wondering if she was angry.

"I'm pregnant!" she announced.

Sonny was overjoyed. He had deeply wanted his own children. He hugged his wife.

In the following fall, Sonny's baby girl was born. Sonny held her close and studied her. The little baby had black hair and dark brown eyes. She had Yupik eyes. For nine months, Sonny had wondered whether the baby would look like her mother or him. His heart swelled as he saw that his baby looked like him, a Yupik. He called her Panik or Bun, which meant baby girl or daughter in Yupik.

Nuliaq seemed disappointed that their daughter did not look at all like her. She held her baby at arm's length and looked at her with a slight frown. It was the first time that Sonny had noticed a coldness in her hitherto beautiful blue eyes. As time went on, Sonny's wife did not nurse the baby. The doctor told her that her blood type was different from her daughter's and breastfeeding would harm the baby. Nuliaq seemed to grow more and more distant every day.

The baby grew and thrived. She was chubby and curly headed. Sonny loved to hold her when he came home from work. He tickled her and thrilled at her bouncy giggles. Bun smiled at him with dimples in her cheeks.

Three years passed swiftly in a rhythm of work and family time. Sonny did not know it at the time but these were the years he would cherish the most in his entire life. Despite the growing distance between Sonny and Nuliaq, his affection for his daughter grew every day. He dreamed of taking his daughter back to Tuckchuck to meet his family. He longed to teach her the Yupik traditions.

Sonny increased his effort to keep close to Nuliaq. He tried to keep their marriage strong in every way he knew how. Nuliaq told him she wanted a house on the waterfront where she could look at the ocean every day. Sonny set his mind to giving his wife her dream house.

Sonny worked hard during the three years. He saved his earnings and bought his wife a house along the beach a small distance from the downtown district of the city of Kodiak. Nuliaq was delighted. She loved to look out the windows at the water and listen to the gentle lapping of the tides. She loved the house but remained distant. She did not want another child. Sonny tried to be understanding.

One evening, Sonny and his family returned from the Good Friday service at the Kodiak Catholic Church. The family was hungry from fasting during the holy day according to the Catholic faith requirements. Sonny had anticipated his family's hunger and sought to cheer them up despite the religious observance. Good Friday was not only a day of fasting which meant only one meal was allowed, but it was also a day of abstinence, which meant that they could only eat fish or seafood and refrain from eating all meat. To make the single meal more exciting, Sonny had earlier brought home several large king crab for dinner. The tasty delicacy met the Good Friday meal requirements.

Sonny and Nuliaq began preparing the meal. Nuliaq set a large pot on the stove full of water. They planned to boil the crab. Sonny fastened his daughter, now a toddler, into her high chair and gave her a piece of cracker to eat as they cooked. At last, the water boiled and Sonny gingerly dropped the enormous crab legs into the steaming pot. He looked at the clock to begin timing the short 10 minutes that the crab needed to boil. It was 5:26 pm. 10 minutes later, he turned off the stove and covered the pot.

Suddenly, the house shook! Nuliaq screamed. Sonny looked over. Bun's high chair was about to tip over! Sonny reached out and held the high chair to prevent Bun from tipping onto the floor. The floor was heaving so much that he could barely stand. Shaking rattled the house.

It was the terrible earthquake of March 27th, 1964.

When the shaking finally subsided, Sonny grabbed coats and boots. He hurriedly dressed Bun and helped Nuliaq out the door. They let the family dog, Spot, loose from his chain. Spot immediately ran towards the road, barking.

Sonny looked at the ocean. The water was beginning to recede from the shores.

The family ran down the long drive from the beachfront house to the road. A car screeched to a halt. It was the bear guide's wife with her two sons! She yelled at them to get in the car. She had heard on the car radio that a tsunami was coming and everyone had to get to higher ground immediately!

Sonny helped his wife and daughter in the car before getting in. The woman gunned the engine and the car flew up the street. She said they were supposed to go to the school which was high enough from the water to be a safe refuge. The street they were on paralleled the slope. A dirt road cut straight up the hill. The woman yanked the wheel and turned up the shortcut. The car jumped forward as she floored the pedal.

The dirt road steepened over a knoll. The bottom of the car caught on the knoll. The tires spun in the dirt. Everyone in the car looked at the woman driving. She pressed on the gas. The tires spun. The engine whined. The tires grabbed purchase and the car bounced wildly up the hill to the school.

Sonny looked at Bun. She was silent, staring with wide eyes. He looked at Nuliaq, she was shaken.

Everyone piled out of the car and into the school. Kodiak officials were ushering people in. The ground shook with the aftershocks of the big earthquake.

Sonny led his family to the school gymnasium. There, a crowd of people was standing at the windows overlooking the ocean below. Sonny, his family and the guide's wife joined the people. The sea water was gone from the shores. Off in the distance they could all see the little island that stood off the harbor.

The guide's wife told Sonny that her husband, his employer, had been out in his boat that day. He was expected back but she did not know where he was. She looked towards the harbor with a white face.

Screams rose from the crowd. A huge black wave rose over the island in the distance! The tsunami slammed into the shores leaving destruction in its path.

Sonny started. He looked around himself. He was still sitting on a bench outside his sister's tent at fish camp on the Yukon River as he reviewed his life. The 1964 earthquake was one of the worst events in his life. He pondered his boyhood again. How had the Yupik traditions of his upbringing and his time in the Guard prepared him for the worst quake in North American history? He thought of his years in the Guard.

Chapter Sixteen

PICKING UP PIECES
1964

SONNY SIGHED DEEPLY AS HIS REVERIE broke and his mind returned to reality at the fish camp. The memories of the Alaska Territorial Guard were those of community. His uncle and Aata joined with all the men of Tuckchuck in forming a unit to protect their village, their Yupik communities along the Yukon and their state. The unity of purpose empowered the Yupik men. Old men dug deep into their remaining strength while young boys grew in purpose and care while serving in the Guard.

Sonny's thoughts returned to the day of the 1964 earthquake on Kodiak Island.

The earthquake had lasted four and a half minutes. It occurred in Prince William Sound to the east and south of Kodiak Island.

The tectonic plates of the Pacific Ocean plate and the North American plate ruptured along a 600 mile seam. Earth was heaved 60 feet up along the rupture zone under the ocean. Land formations were thrust up 30 feet in places on Kodiak Island. It was the second largest quake recorded in the world.

Tsunamis were generated throughout Alaska. Tsunamis slammed the coasts of California, Oregon, Washington and British Columbia. The waves reached thousands of miles across the Pacific to the shores of Hawaii and Japan. Tsunamis destroyed many coastal communities along the extensive Alaskan coast line.

Sonny did not know the scientific facts of the quake but he was shaken to the core. As he stared in horror at the tsunami wave that crashed onto the city of Kodiak, he knew that many people would die that day. Later, when the destruction was measured, 131 souls were lost that day. On nearby Afognak Island, the native village of Afognak was completely destroyed by the waves.

The residents of Kodiak who had escaped to the high ground of the school stood in a frightened huddle. Sonny gathered himself. He moved Nuliaq aside and placed their daughter in her arms. He told Nuliaq to remain safe in the school. He needed to go down into the city of Kodiak and help with the rescue effort. Nuliaq numbly nodded her head and gripped Bun tightly. She begged him to be careful and return safely. He assured her with a grim nod that he would be safe and left. His heart pounded and he did not know what death and destruction he would find in the tsunami's aftermath.

A man had a pickup truck parked outside the school. He called to the men gathering outside to jump in the truck and go with him to see who needed rescue. Sonny joined the men. They huddled in the back of the truck. Night was drawing near. The faces of each man was wan and grim.

The man drove his truck down the street from the school towards the downtown district. He drove a few blocks into downtown Kodiak before parking the truck. Debris lay everywhere. Aftershocks from the earthquake shook the ground and continued to shake over the next hours.

Sonny walked with the men into the downtown. Kodiak was unrecognizable. Boats lay strewn across the streets and against houses. The wave had carried them from the harbor into the city and dumped them in disarray across the streets as the flood water receded. Big vessels lay on their sides. Logs, barrels, fishing equipment littered the streets. A fire sputtered near a building.

All night and half of the next day, Sonny helped the rescue teams look for survivors. He helped carry the wounded to the pickup to be taken up the mountain to the hospital. The trauma first aid training Sonny had learned from being in the Guard as a boy proved invaluable as he set broken legs and helped bind up wounds. Sonny worked with the teams of men, carrying lights and calling out for survivors.

Sonny looked carefully for his employer, the bear hunting guide. He could not find the boat among the wreckage. He began to ask men if they knew where the bear guide was. At last, one injured man told Sonny as he and the other rescuers carried him to the truck to take to the hospital that the guide had gone out on the ocean early in the day. The guide was still at sea.

The night passed and the dawn arrived gray and misty. Sonny made his way back to the school. Nuliaq was waiting anxiously for him. The guide's wife sought him out as he walked into the school. He told her that her husband was out on the water and had not yet returned. She was tense with worry. He tried to reassure her that the guide was safest out on the water where the tsunami was not a danger to vessels. He described the state of destruction at the boat harbor and lay down. Sonny closed his eyes and thought how grateful he was that the Yupik people lived far away from the tsunami's danger. He was soon fast asleep.

Sonny slept until late afternoon. He went down the hill to his house on the beach front below. The beach front house that had been the dream home of his wife was gone. Only a broken concrete foundation remained under mud and debris. He felt a sense of emptiness as he trudged back up the hill to the school. He found Spot waiting for him on the hill. He brought the dog back to the school and found food and water for him. Bun hugged the dog and stayed by his side. She was quiet and wide-eyed.

The next day, Sonny and Nuliaq decided to walk down to their house together. Sonny carried Bun as they descended the hill from the school. The view of the low land that lay before them looked unrecognizable. Nuliaq wept as she stood on the broken house's foundation. Bun was confused. She asked over and over again why they could not go home. She wanted to go home. The toddler could not comprehend that the house was gone. She looked at Sonny as if expecting him to put the house back and make everything right again. When Sonny explained that the house was gone, she asked where it went. Bun looked from her crying mother to Sonny with big eyes. Sonny finally sat on a log and waited until Nuliaq stopped crying.

Sonny and Nuliaq talked a moment. They decided to search the beach to look for any of their belongings that might have survived the tsunami.

Sonny carried Bun as he and Nuliaq walked down the beach. Nuliaq wiped the tears that kept welling up in her eyes. A torrent of words gave voice to her misery that had been building up and now gushed forth as she viewed the destruction around her. She said that the house was the only thing in her life that made her happy. She had not wanted to have Bun. She did not like how she had to quit working as a nurse at the hospital to stay home with Bun.

Three weeks ago, in early March, Sonny's wife had received an urgent telegram. Her brother had been killed in while serving in Vietnam. She had taken the news hard. For long hours, she looked out the front window of their home, watching the tide rise and fall. She told Sonny that watching the tide everyday made her understand that life must go on. The beachfront home was where she found comfort in her sorrow. Now, the tsunami had completely wiped away the one part of her life that she cherished most, the beachfront house.

After a half mile of walking, Sonny and his wife started to find some of their possessions strewn along the beach. The house itself was nowhere in sight. Sonny set Bun down as he helped Nuliaq pick up boxes of photo albums that were mercifully spared from destruction. A baby blanket of Bun's lay on the rocks. The couple made a pile of everything they could find from their home. Sonny told his wife he would come back down with a large sack and gather the pile to carry up to the school. The couple sadly trudged back up the hill. Spot followed along with his tail hanging low. Bun had fallen silent. She no longer asked any questions.

When Sonny and his family got back to the school, they found it bustling with activity. The Navy had mobilized on the island. Food and blankets were brought to the gymnasium. More people had come to the school seeking shelter.

Sonny settled Nuliaq and Bun in the school gym with a bed of blankets. He went to the kitchen and asked for several trash bags. He returned to the beach at dusk. Filling his trash bags with the pile of recovered belongings, he made his way back to the school.

He spoke with other people who had gone searching through the debris during the day as he passed them along the beach. They wearily made their way back to the school for the night.

The days passed. Easter Sunday Mass was held in the gym.

News of the destruction and devastation of the earthquake and tsunamis began to pour in on the news reports on the radio. Though March ended and April began, the spring seemed depressed and full of fear. A dark cloud of gloom seemed to hang over the island.

Sonny felt uneasy. He tried to understand what he was feeling. He felt a deep sense of gratitude that his family was safe and that not one of them had been killed or injured in the disaster of the earthquake. He talked to people as he went about looking for ways to help in the recovery. People were shaken. Some were grateful to be alive. Others were full of despair and doom.

As the island and city of Kodiak struggled to recover from the disaster, the homeless were given trailers to live in. One day, Sonny's wife told him that they had to talk. They waited until Bun was napping before they talked. Sonny told Nuliaq he was sure he could find work helping to move the big boats back in the water by operating large equipment. She hesitated a moment before she said what was on her mind. She hated the trailer. She wanted a home and land. The sea had been her love, but now she wanted to live far away from the sea and the danger of tsunamis. A friend of hers was married to a man who owned mines. The husband knew of a place they could move to near Fairbanks in the middle of Alaska. They could be caretakers of a mining camp over the winter. They could live free in a cabin with a check for supplies to cover their winter food needs. After the winter was over, Sonny would be paid for the full season of caretaking until the mine opened in the early spring. Sonny could trap and earn extra money from the furs. Sonny studied her blue eyes. He agreed to take the offer.

SONNY CHUCKLED TO HIMSELF AS HE shifted his weight on the bench at fish camp. He thought of his wife's blue eyes and how he felt thrilled to be married to a woman with blue eyes. How many times did he ask himself how lucky a simple Yupik man was to be married to a woman with blue eyes?

Then, Sonny grew serious. He looked at the fish camp yard before him. He had come full circle, and his thoughts drifted back to his youth and to the days of the Guard.

Chapter Seventeen

WOLF TALE
1965

SONNY AND NULIAQ DECIDED TO SELL the Jeep which had miracu-lously survived the tsunami. The money would pay for airplane tickets from Kodiak to Anchorage, the largest city in Alaska. In Anchorage, they hoped that the rest of the money left over from the sale of the Jeep would be enough to buy another vehicle. Then, they planned to drive to Fairbanks for the caretaker job at the mining camp.

The Jeep sold quickly.

Sonny's wife packed quickly, too. It was late August 1964 now. She wanted to move from Kodiak and settle in the Fairbanks area before winter set in. She had heard that the winters in Interior Alaska were a lot colder than the ones in Kodiak. The temperatures could fall to 60 degrees below zero Fahrenheit.

Sonny assured her that he had experienced the extreme cold and long dark days of winter in its harshest challenge while grow-ing up along the lower Yukon River. He knew what furs were warmest to wear.

The trip to Anchorage went smoothly. The friend of Sonny's wife arranged lodging for Sonny and his family in the city at the expense of the mining company. Sonny and Nuliaq hired a taxi to take them to the automotive dealer. The car salesman shook his head when he learned how much money they had to buy another vehicle. It was not enough to buy a truck or another Jeep. After scratching his head a few minutes, the salesman waved them to the back parking lot. There was an older station wagon. It was not pretty but it was solid and dependable. The salesman took their money, gave them the title, sales slip and keys. Sonny drove the car to their lodging while Bun sat on his wife's lap. Spot panted and wagged his tail as he rode in the back seat.

The drive to Fairbanks was almost 400 miles from Anchorage. Sonny and Nuliaq packed food and blankets in the station wagon. Spot rode on the top of the piles of their belongings. They took turns driving long days. The family rarely encountered other travelers driving the highway. They stopped to cook a meal and slept the night in the station wagon. The nights were still fairly warm, so the trip was pleasant and exciting.

When Sonny arrived in Fairbanks, Nuliaq directed him to an office. They met with the mining company representative. The representative had papers for them to sign as an agreement for pay and grubstake supplies. The grubstake supplies were food, traps and other necessities paid for by the mining company ahead of the caretaker season to provide for the needs of whoever they hired to watch the mining camp. The representative sent Sonny to a supplier where they picked up their winter supplies.

The station wagon was loaded down with their possessions and a winter's worth of supplies. Sonny and his family drove out to the mining camp to settle in for the season. The camp was located about 50 miles north of Fairbanks along a gravel road. They drove over a mountain summit until the road dropped down to a creek that fed into a nearby river.

The camp consisted of a cook house, bunk house, garage and

supply house. There were several small sheds for equipment storage. At the edge of the camp was a larger cabin, which was the caretaker or watchman's residence. Sonny and Nuliaq parked the station wagon in front of the cabin and began unloading. Spot leapt off the car and began sniffing everywhere with his tail wagging as he went. Bun napped in the back seat of the car.

The camp lay nestled amongst hills that rose on all its sides. The hills were covered in birch and spruce stands. The birch leaves were bright yellow and contrasted with the dark green of the spruce. The creek ran in babbling currents down to the river. The river itself was tiny compared to the Yukon, but it was placid and deep. On either side of the river, up and down the valley among the hills, were beaver ponds surrounded by willows. The willows were stubby and stunted from being browsed by moose during the winter.

As Bun woke from her nap during the long drive out to the camp, Sonny finished unloading. His wife began unpacking their belongings in the cabin, while Sonny checked the stoves. There were two of them in the cabin. One was a round barrel stove for heating. It stood almost in the center of the cabin. The other stove was against a wall. It was smaller with a flat top for cooking and an oven beside the burner box. They both looked to be in good condition.

Sonny picked up Bun to carry her outside with him. There was a lean to shed against the cabin for cut wood, and there was already some wood stacked in it. Sonny looked around. At the far edge of the yard was a large pile of logs. Next to the pile was a saw horse. Near the saw horse was a big chopping block for splitting wood. Sonny smiled at Bun and told her that there was plenty of wood for the winter. She smiled back.

Sonny explored the tool shed. He found several saws and axes among the tools. He felt satisfied that the wood supply for heating the cabin and cooking their meals was well stocked. He was relieved he did not have to go into the woods and fell trees for fuel. It would be hard to haul the logs back to the saw horse.

Sonny returned to the cabin. Nuliaq already had the cabin looking comfortable and welcoming. She was humming as she worked. Spot lay on a blanket in the corner and wagged his tail as Sonny and Bun entered.

Sonny began unpacking the boxes of grub. There were wooden boards nailed to the wall that provided shelves for a pantry. More boards served as a table for mixing bread or washing dishes along the wall. Several pots and cast iron pans hung on the wall behind the cook stove. Two large metal basins were under the table that served as a counter. The basins were for washing the dishes.

By evening, the little cabin was bright and warm. The aroma of fresh baking bread filled the air. A stew bubbled in the pot on the cook stove. Kerosene lamps lit the cabin interior. Bun had been bathed in a small metal tub from the tool shed and was waiting patiently for her dinner. She sat on the floor and petted Spot.

The family ate their first meal in their new home. Sonny felt a sense of relief as he looked at Nuliaq. She was tucking Bun into her small wooden bunk next to their bed. Spot licked Sonny's hand. The cabin was peaceful as they settled in for the night.

Life at the mining camp was busy. The seasons changed quickly. Winter came. Snows fell deep. The cold was bitter and dangerous, but the cabin stayed warm and cozy. Sonny and Nuliaq worked from morning until night. The wood needed to be sawed and chopped and hauled into the cabin every day. Sonny's wife cooked, baked bread, washed their clothes and prepared their baths. Despite the cold and isolation, she was cheerful as she worked. She loved the beauty of the land around them and pointed out the things she loved in their new surroundings.

Sonny had made another pair of snowshoes when the snows started to fall. When the ponds and river froze, he laid out a trap line for beaver, lynx, fox, marten, mink and wolverine. He took the animals he harvested in his traps into one of the equipment buildings, which had a small wood stove and lanterns in it, and skinned them by the light of the lamp. He stretched their hides over wire stretchers and hung them to dry in the warmth of the cabin. When the hides were dry, he stacked them neatly in a great wooden box at the end of the room.

By December, Sonny was pleased by the size of the fur pile he had harvested. The land around the mining camp was full of fur-bearing animals. The beavers in particular were a tasty addition to their meals as well.

January was even colder. The snow quit falling and the skies cleared. The bitter chill tried to creep in through the corners of the cabin. Their window panes were heavily frosted. When Sonny went outside, he had to cover himself completely to avoid frostbite. His wife and Bun were stuck inside the cabin for fear of freezing.

Then in mid-January, the moon waxed full. The cold was at its worst, but the brightness of the moon on the snow was almost as bright as midday. Sonny had to get up several times at night to put logs on the fire in the wood stove so that the cabin would not freeze. Bun, Nuliaq and Spot lay buried under blankets.

One night after Sonny fed the fire, he paused to look out the window at the sparkling snow under the moon. He suddenly stiffened. Something big was moving through the yard!

Sonny carefully and silently scrapped some frost off the pane to get a better look. It was a huge wolf! Then, he caught his breath. There was another wolf! The larger wolf was the male and the smaller female followed him as they sniffed around the yard. Sonny watched the wolves until they were out of sight. Concerned, he went back to bed.

The next morning, Sonny told Nuliaq about the wolves as he sipped his coffee. He made sure Bun was still sleeping before he spoke. Nuliaq listened with fear growing in her eyes. When Sonny finished, she frowned as she silently fixed the breakfast meal. They agreed not to frighten Bun by refraining from talking about the wolves in front of her.

Sonny ate and went outside. He carried his rifle and spoke sharply to Spot as the dog ran out. The dog raced around sniffing and barking. After Spot had toileted himself, Sonny put him back in the cabin and began to survey the yard. He tracked the wolves around the buildings. The wolves had done no damage. The wolf tracks left the yard and crossed the creek. He squinted at the hill. The wolves must have retreated up the hill for the day to a spot on the hill above the camp where they could watch what was going on below. The pair must have found a place to bed down for the day.

When Bun was napping, Sonny told Nuliaq of his plan for the coming night. The building he used for skinning what he caught on his trap line had a window that looked across the yard. He could see the front of the cabin from the window. He planned to knock out one of the little squares of the window panes to put his rifle muzzle through. He would build a fire in the building and sit at the window all night watching for a chance to shoot the wolves. Sonny was sure the wolf hides would provide a lot of much needed money. Nuliaq understood the opportunity. She still felt a twinge of fear that the wolves would harm them in some way. Sonny assured her that they were safe.

After Bun was safely tucked in bed, Sonny checked the supply of wood for the cabin stove for the frigid night. He made sure Nuliaq was ready to tend to the stove through the night to keep the cabin warm. He told her not come outside. There was a spare rifle in the cabin but he assured her that it would not be needed. He made sure the spare rifle was loaded and leaning safely to the side of the door in case of an emergency. Then, he bundled up and stepped outside with his own rifle.

The cold made Sonny catch his breath as he walked quickly and stealthily to the building where he skinned the animals. He locked the door behind him and lit the kerosene lamp. His breath hung in ice crystals in the air. Sonny lit the fire and waited for it to warm the building. When the building was warm and the fire banked with logs, he extinguished the kerosene lamp. He took his place at the window.

Earlier in the day, Sonny had gently wiggled a square piece of the pane loose enough to slide out. He removed the pane. The air was bitter as it flowed in through the window. Sonny pulled his mittens back on. He placed the tip of his rifle through the hole. He had a woolen blanket which he drew around him over his coat. He would be warm enough for the long night ahead.

Outside, the yard was fully illuminated by the moon overhead. Above the hills to the north was the faint outline of the northern lights dancing across the sky. They were outshone by the great round moon. The hills and the little valley lay still.

Sonny looked through the window across the yard towards the cabin. He chuckled to himself as he recognized his wife's pale face peering out the window. He wondered if she could see him. He gave a little wave. Her head bobbed. Sonny hoped she would stay quietly and safely in the cabin as he had told her. He turned his attention to surveying the yard.

The hours dragged by. Sonny stiffly rose and built the fire up in the wood stove. He warmed himself a moment before returning to the window and resumed his vigil.

The wolves did not show that night. The next day, Sonny was tired. He cut and chopped wood. He wearily hauled the wood into the cabin and the building he had spent the night in. He hauled water for the cabin. In the afternoon, after lunch, he napped in the cabin as Bun played with Spot nearby on the floor.

When Sonny woke from his nap, he gratefully accepted the coffee Nuliaq offered him. He scanned the sky outside the window. The cold weather was not letting up. Just then, there was a distant howl from the hill above!

Spot barked as Bun gave a little scream of surprise. Sonny quieted Spot and picked up Bun. He explained to her that the howl was from a wolf. He told her about wolves in an amusing way so as not to frighten her. She listened with solemn dark eyes.

When the night came, Sonny returned to the out building for another night of hunting the wolves through the window. He blew on his fingers after lighting the stove. The night was colder than the previous.

Sonny had taken a second thick woolen blanket from the bunk house to wrap himself in as he waited at the window. He draped the blanket over his rifle to make sure it was not too frozen to fire when he shot the wolves.

After three long hours, the wolves walked into the yard. They came one at a time. The massive male led the way. He sniffed at the buildings as he advanced. After a few minutes, the female followed. She smelled the same buildings as the male in imitation. She paused every second step and looked around the yard. The wolves were the largest Sonny had ever seen!

Sonny leaned forward and pulled the blankets out of the way. He lowered his head to the sights of the rifle. He aimed the rifle at the male. The wolf moved to the center of the yard and stood. Sonny tracked the wolf with his sight. It was the perfect shot. He held his breath and carefully pulled the trigger. Pow!

The male wolf fell over. The female jumped back. She stood looking at the fallen body of the male a long moment. Then, she looked around the buildings as if trying to figure out where the killer was. Sonny slipped to one knee to aim the rifle at her. The female was standing at the edge of the yard.

Suddenly, the curtains were pulled back from the cabin window. Sonny's wife began scraping the frost off the window. She was trying to see what had happened because she had been startled awake by the shot. Then, Sonny heard a muffled cry. Bun had been wakened by the firing of the rifle and the sound of her mother going to the window. Sonny's wife disappeared from the window. She had gone to attend to Bun and stop the toddler's crying.

The female wolf turned at the sounds in the cabin. She disappeared in an instant.

Sonny waited several minutes to see if the female would return. He heard a mournful howl far off on the hill above the camp. The female had fled up the hill.

Sonny returned the pane of window into its square. The frigid flow of air stopped. He stood a moment by the wood stove to warm his hands. Then, he stepped outside to the yard.

The male wolf was dead. Sonny pulled the legs as he dragged it to the building. The wolf was heavy. Sonny guessed the male's weight to be at least 175 pounds or more. Its paws seemed plate-sized.

After carefully storing the wolf in the outbuilding, Sonny latched the door. He crossed the yard with his rifle to the cabin. After he knocked a moment, Nuliaq opened the door. He assured her that the other wolf was long gone. The female would not return tonight.

Sonny told Nuliaq and Bun about shooting the male wolf. Then finally, in the early hours of the morning, he slept.

SONNY CHUCKLED TO HIMSELF AS HE sat at fish camp. His wife had taken a picture of him with the wolf that winter long ago. The wolf hide had brought them a lot of money. Nuliaq was pleased and proud.

The female wolf never returned to the camp. He trapped her a month later. She was smaller but her pelt was in good condition. Her furs had also provided a lot of money.

Chapter Eighteen

Victory Redux
1965

Sonny's thoughts returned to the present as he sat on the bench at fish camp. He thought of the time when he had been the gold mine caretaker near Fairbanks in the 1960s. The success of shooting the immense wolf was a victory.

However, the victory of shooting the wolf was no different than the victory of World War II. It was a victory that was bittersweet. It was a victory that heralded changes in Sonny's life that he could not avoid and that he would not have made if he had had a choice. Just like the struggle with overcoming tuberculosis that he had to fight to recover while everyone else was celebrating the end of World War II, the struggle of everyday life to be a satisfactory husband and father challenged him personally as the world rushed forward around him. Life held some greater difficulties than tuberculosis.

Alaska progressed in the new decades after World War II as the boom and bust of industries and get rich quick plots played for the development of the state's vast natural resources. Alaska became the 49th state in the Union. The Alaska Territorial Guard and the Native heroes were quickly forgotten.

Sonny sighed deeply. It was the regretful sigh of a dying man. He returned to his thoughts of his life at the gold mine that winter north of Fairbanks.

THE WINTER TURNED BRUTAL. THE THERMOMETERS on the outside of the mining camp buildings read -60 Fahrenheit. That was the bottom of the mercury reading. It was impossible to tell how much colder the temperature actually was, but it was painfully cold.

Sonny made a pair of mittens out of the beaver hide. He wrapped skins around his feet in his boots. With the warm fur, he was able to continue checking his traps through the cold weather the remainder of January and into February.

The cold weather drove the fur bearing animals down into the river valley, and the animals eagerly sought out the scents he used with his traps. The fur of the animals he found in the traps was luxuriant from the cold, thick and in good condition. Sonny kept busy with the traps, skinning and drying out the hides.

Sonny's wife had to remain in the cabin with Bun because of the lethal cold spell. As the days passed, the cabin grew tense. Bun fell silent and sat in the corner playing with the dog. Sonny's wife had grown impatient and on edge. Cabin fever for Sonny's wife gave way to baking and cooking. Nuliaq's irritation from being housebound with a toddler hung in the air of the cabin. She fussed at him to fill the wood box before he left to check traps. Keeping the wood stoves fueled was constant work for Sonny whenever he was not tending to the traps and furs. The tension in the cabin became so thick that Sonny would leave for his trap line in relief.

When Sonny returned to the cabin in the evening after his work, Nuliaq would apologize for her outbursts. She spread the table with fresh bread and delicious meals. The evenings passed in peace until the next morning.

Sonny began a daily habit of eating his dinner and helping to wash the dishes. Then, he got on the floor to play with Bun. It was his favorite time of the day.

The little toddler spent her days without speaking to anyone beside the dog. Her face lit up when Sonny knelt next to her. He often found she had made little toys of pieces of wood which she held up to him with a giggle. He asked her questions and acted out stories with the little makeshift toys until bed time.

Sonny stared into the darkness one night after playing with Bun. He thought of his childhood in Tuckchuck. It was such a rich life full of his parents, grandparents, aunts, uncles, cousins and elders. Sadness stabbed his heart as he realized Bun was too isolated in the little cabin with no one to play with besides a dog. Instead of gentle kindness, Bun only received firm correction from her mother. Tears burned his eyes. This was not the Yupik way to raise a child.

The next morning, Sonny tried to talk to his wife about his concerns for Bun. She grew stiff as he struggled to find words in English to explain how he worried that Bun was too isolated. Her blue eyes grew cold. Sonny felt a chill in his heart. He had never directly experienced the coldness of her eyes before.

Sonny's wife began to answer him speaking in a hard voice. The life at the mining camp was the most beautiful and happiest life she had felt like living in a long, long time. The safe distance from the ocean and dangers of tsunamis gave her security. The freedom from all the problems of city life was what she had always wanted. The luxury of having the entire valley to herself was what she came to Alaska to find and now she had finally found it.

Sonny's wife looked at Bun, who was listening from her corner with large frightened eyes. She said that she thought Bun was better off here without other children to bother her. She continued to say that Bun was an Alaskan. Bun was born to live like a true Alaskan and being isolated in the cabin at the mining camp was the best thing for her. Bun was free to be a carefree child.

Sonny kept silent. He had never argued with Nuliaq. He had never realized his wife had such a hard heart. He left to check his traps.

All day long, as Sonny walked along his trap line, he thought about his wife and daughter. He thought about his grandparents and Aata and Aana. The Yupik way of life was a way of peace, understanding, kindness and taking care of one another. Men and women knew their roles and helped each other raise a family. The extended family helped and was considered immediate family. A cousin wasn't a cousin. A cousin was a brother. The elders talked to the young and the children listened respectively. Bun had no elders to talk to her. He wondered if Bun was lonely.

Sonny thought about Nuliaq. He knew she was not Yupik but he struggled to understand her. He had thought their love would stand the challenges that life would throw at them. Life in Alaska was harsh, difficult and dangerous. However, if a man and woman loved each other and worked together, they could make a good home and raise a family so their love grew with each new child.

It was sad that Nuliaq did not want more children. Bun would always be alone. Sonny searched the teachings of his Yupik elders for ways to help Bun overcome loneliness and isolation. He decided to teach her what he had learned of his Yupik ways. It would not be easy. Bun was not learning to naturally speak Yupik because her mother only spoke English. Sonny spoke broken English. Sonny sighed. He could not read more than a handful of words.

Sonny looked down at his snowshoes. He could make things. He could teach Bun as he showed her how to make the useful things he had learned to make as a Yupik boy.

As Sonny recalled his boyhood, he recalled the years he spent in the Territorial Guard with the men. As Sonny reset the last trap in his trap line, he thought to himself that being in the Guard had changed everything. The Guard and the war had opened a door to a world beyond his Yupik life. He had eagerly gone through the door and left his family, village and Yupik culture. He had set out on a journey and he would see it through until the end. He loved his little family and he would try hard to make everything turn out right.

When Sonny got home, he worked hard to skin the animals from his traps. It was late when he finished and wearily returned to the cabin. Upon entering, he found the cabin, bright, full of delicious smells and peaceful. Nuliaq was on the bed with Bun. She looked up and smiled.

Bun sat up and said excitedly, "Daddy, you're home! I missed you!" The toddler slid off the bed and ran to her father. She reached her arms out for him to pick her up. "Daddy, Mom is reading a book to me! It is a story about a fox!"

Sonny held Bun tight and smiled back at Nuliaq.

His wife had brought several children's books from Kodiak when they moved. She had found them in the pile of boxes in the corner. This was the first night of what became a new bedtime routine of reading to Bun. Sonny listened as Nuliaq read while dozing off and on. The stories were not like Yupik stories but he found them interesting all the same.

Life in the cabin during the cold fell into a new rhythm, and the irritated mood hanging in the air disappeared.

At long last, the cold spell broke during the last week of February. As March began, snow storms arrived. Three feet of snow fell overnight during the first week of March. Another three feet of snow descended a few days later.

When Sonny started the job of caretaker at the mine, he was told by the mining representatives that the road to the mine would be plowed clear of snow by late March. The plan was for Sonny to drive to Fairbanks in late March to bring the furs he trapped and dried over the winter to town to sell. The food and supplies that the mining office had provided were enough to last Sonny and his family until late March. When Sonny drove into Fairbanks in March, he would be provided with more supplies by the mining company if he needed them. By late April, the miners would return to the camp and Sonny's job of caretaking the mine was done for the season.

In early March as the snow fell, Sonny and his wife inventoried their remaining supplies and food. Everything was running out. They were filled with concern. The deep snow changed their plan for the trip to Fairbanks. The snow plow could not open the road for them to drive into Fairbanks.

Sonny knew that hunting moose or other animals in the deep snow would be similarly impossible. The snow was too deep to snowshoe far enough to find any animal worth hunting.

So Sonny packed a small rifle to hunt ptarmigan and rabbits as he went to check his traps. He wore a rucksack because he planned to pull his traps for the spring. He donned his snowshoes and began the arduous journey through his trap line. The traps were empty for the first time that winter. He sprung his traps and packed as many of them as he could back to the mining camp. He kept a careful eye out for any animal to shoot for food. The land seemed barren of life under the deep snow.

Sonny returned home late. He was exhausted as he hung his snowshoes up and headed into the cabin. Bun was already sleeping soundly in her little bed.

Nuliaq placed bread and a bowl of stew on the table before him. She whispered that it was the last of the flour and stew meat. All that was left was a can of milk and a half jar of sugar. She whispered worriedly to Sonny that they needed to find food.

Sonny nodded. He ate slowly. He told Nuliaq about the traps and that he was very tired. Sonny told her they would try to drive to Fairbanks to get food the next day. He had a plan.

Sonny immediately fell asleep that night. He woke in the morning, his stomach growling as he lay awake thinking about his plan to drive to Fairbanks. He wished fervently for a steaming cup of strong coffee.

The day was warm. The bright sun rose over the hills, and the snow began to melt, becoming heavy and dense. Instead of six feet of light fluffy snow, there was only three feet of wet snow. As the morning passed, the snow on the road melted to two feet thick. It was wetter and heavier.

Sonny was relieved that the car started. His wife packed the station wagon with some blankets. The couple had decided to leave the furs Sonny had harvested from the trap line over the winter to make room for two heavy metal cans of spare gas to replenish the car. Sonny packed his rifle under the blankets in case they had an opportunity to shoot a moose and feast on it over an open fire.

As Sonny shoveled the car out, Nuliaq settled Bun and the dog in the car. The plan was for Sonny to snowshoe down the road on one side. Then, he would snowshoe back to the car and drive it forward along the snowshoe tracks.

It was midmorning when Sonny and his family left the camp.

The first 10 miles of the road were mostly flat as it followed the river. Sonny made good time as he used his snowshoes to make a way in the snow for the car to drive through. His stomach growled as he worked. The sun was hot above him and reflected brightly off the snow. The valley was strangely quiet until midafternoon, when a flock of chickadees flew across the road. They twittered cheerily in the March air.

The 10 miles of flat road turned into a slow uphill grade away from the river bottom. The increasing incline began to tax Sonny's strength as he tramped through the snow on his snowshoes. The snow was becoming deeper as the road climbed.

As perspiration poured from his brow and his stomach demanded food, Sonny concentrated on his task of clearing a path for the car. His thoughts became disciplined as he had learned from his Yupik elders. He glanced back. Bun was hungry too. He had to do whatever it took to get his daughter to food and safety.

In late afternoon, when Sonny reached the car to drive it forward, Nuliaq handed him a jar. He drank the contents eagerly. It was weak sugar water. He wiped his brow and paused a moment. Refreshed, he took his snowshoes off and drove the car forward down the track he had made.

The arduous journey continued until twilight. The family had made it to the final slope leading up to the summit of the ridge. Halfway up the mountain side, the daylight gave out. Sonny looked around. He found some scraggly spruce trees for wood. He took an ax from the car and began to chop wood for a fire.

As the sun set, the temperature plummeted. It was the time of year when the temperature varied as much as 70 degrees between daytime highs and nighttime lows.

The overnight temperatures at the mining camp had been -15 degrees Fahrenheit. During the day, the high temperature was just above freezing. Today had been a warm sunny day with the snow melting in the radiance.

Sonny guessed the temperature that night would drop to 20 below. The car was parked halfway up the mountain on the north side. The sun did not reach the north side of the mountain along the road at all during the day. A slight breeze chilled them to the bone.

Sonny chopped enough wood for them to burn through the night. He stacked it near the car for easy grabbing. He was worried that if they ran the car for warmth during the night, they would run out of gas before they reached help.

Sonny built the fire near the back of the car. It warmed the interior some. His wife gave Bun some of the canned milk diluted with water. There was a small piece of bread left for each of them. Sonny and his wife drank small sips of sugar water and slowly chewed the bread.

The awareness of the need to get to help the next day hung over them unspoken. Bun fell asleep with the dog lying near her in the car. Sonny felt bad for the dog who was as hungry as the rest of the family. He could see how devoted the dog was to his daughter as he looked at the pair sleeping together for warmth.

Sonny built the fire up to warm the car. Nuliaq whispered a question to him. She asked if wolves might come and bother them. He replied that he did not think wolves were near. He had not seen any sign of any animals all day. It was as if the road was abandoned of all life except little birds that were too small to shoot and eat.

They closed the car up for the night. Sonny's wife bundled up in the back of the station wagon and fell asleep. Sonny sat up a while. He fed the fire as he warmed his aching muscles. It had been a hard day. If he could take a steam bath, the soreness of his muscles and joints would be relieved. Finally, Sonny felt certain that no wolves were near after watching and listening. He crawled into the station wagon alongside Nuliaq and daughter. The night air was bitterly cold.

Sonny slept deeply in spite of the cold. Suddenly, he woke confused. He could hear Bun crying. Something was very wrong. Bun was crying weakly between gasps for air. Sonny struggled to open his eyes. He wanted to fall back asleep and it was extremely difficult for him to move.

The car was running! Sonny became aware of the engine noise through the fog of his brain. Next to him, his wife lay immobile. They needed air.

Sonny fought with all his might. He moved his fingers to the window handle. It took more strength to turn the handle. The window cracked. It was the hardest thing he had ever done in his life. Cold air gushed in the tiny crack. After a moment, Sonny found strength to sit up. He leaned forward and turned the key in the car's ignition. The engine stopped.

After several minutes, Sonny felt his lungs breathing and his head clearing. He unrolled the window fully. Bun began to gulp in air between pitiful cries. The dog whined. Sonny shook his wife's shoulder. She did not respond.

Sonny reached across the back of the station wagon to unroll the other window. The crisp air filled the car. Bun stopped crying and lay whimpering. The dog jumped out of the window and began to eat snow.

Sonny shook Nuliaq's shoulder again. She barely stirred. He uncovered her face and studied her. After a few minutes, she opened her eyes. She looked confused. Sonny told her that the car had been running. The tail pipe had most likely been blocked by snow. The air in the station wagon had become saturated with carbon monoxide. He told her how Bun's crying had saved them.

The sky was turning light in the east. Sonny put on his boots and went out to start the fire again. His head hurt. After a time, Nuliaq and Bun joined him. Nuliaq explained that she had awakened. She saw that the sky was getting light. She wanted to warm the car up a little before they woke up, so she started it. She must have fallen back to sleep or succumbed to the vapors to become incapacitated. She had intended to shut the car off after a few minutes of warming the engine.

It was a grim morning. The sun rose but did not shine on the road on their side of the mountain. Sonny and his wife had headaches. Sonny warmed some sugar water and they all drank it with the last of the bread. Sonny let the fire burn out and got ready to begin their journey to town again.

Sonny donned his snowshoes and tamped down a track a short ways up the road. It was steep and curvy along this part of the road. He made his way back to the car. The snow depth was greater here. The car's tires spun as he drove forward in the snow shoe tracks.

After a few hours, it became apparent that the snow was becoming too deep for the car to drive over the summit. Sonny was exhausted and nauseated. Nuliaq felt the same. Bun had retreated into herself again and sat in the back quietly. She held the dog tightly as she peered out of a bundle of blankets.

The car reached a quarter mile from the summit. The road was blocked by a massive snow drift. Sonny stared at the drift in dumb weariness. He looked back at the car. He realized that the only way for the car to drive through the drift was if he shoveled a way out. The task was daunting. He had packed a shovel, but it seemed like a toothpick in relation to the snow drift. He was tired. He snowshoed back to the car and explained to Nuliaq what needed to be done if they were going to drive on. She offered to help take turns with the shovel.

Sonny rested awhile as he sat in the car.

Suddenly, there was a sound!

A huge snow plow appeared over the summit above them!

The plow hit the drift and stopped.

Sonny and his wife jumped out of the car and yelled.

The plow engine cut. Soon, a man peered down at them. He looked astonished.

Sonny felt a flush of victory over the whole situation. His family was safe now.

After Sonny and his family climbed through the snow to the plow, the driver told them how amazed he was to see them. He exclaimed how skinny and gaunt they all looked. He explained that the mining company had told him that the road needed to be opened. The mining company was worried that the caretaker and his family might be running out of supplies and need food. So, the mining company had called the road department crew to send a snow plow out to clear the road to the mining camp and check on the family to see if they were safe.

The snow plow driver was becoming increasingly concerned as he drove out of Fairbanks in his pickup the previous day. The road maintenance station was several miles out of Fairbanks, so the driver parked his truck at the station and started plowing the road towards the mining camp. The first day, the driver was able to plow half way up the summit. The snow was wet and difficult to plow on the south slope of the mountain that faced the warm sun. The driver had to put chains on his plow to keep the tires from sliding in the wet snow when it became packed under the plow.

The driver returned the next day early. He was determined to reach the mining camp the same day. He was worried that the family might be in serious trouble by now since the snow was so deep. It was a difficult job to get the road cleared to the summit. The snow was much deeper at the summit than on the lower part of the mountain.

Sonny and his family rode with the driver in the plow back down the mountain to where his pickup was parked. The driver left his plow and loaded the family into his pickup. He drove them into Fairbanks to the mining company office.

The mining company hastily paid Sonny and helped him find a place to stay for the night with his family. Food was brought to them and they gratefully ate.

The next day, Sonny returned with the snowplow driver. After the drift was plowed, Sonny drove the station wagon into Fairbanks. The following day, he rode with the snowplow driver in his pickup to return to the camp to gather the furs he had trapped over the winter to sell. Sonny was paid by the fur trader for all the hides he had trapped over the winter.

Finally, Sonny rested. He had a good pay check from the mining company for taking care of the camp over the winter, and he had very good pay for the furs he had trapped. The fur buyer remarked that the furs were the best quality he had ever seen. Sonny and Nuliaq were happy and Bun was safe.

The accommodations provided by the mining company consisted of a small house near the mining office where workers stayed before they left for the camp. It was comfortable and warm. There was a small but efficient kitchen. Nuliaq was delighted.

The house also had an indoor bathroom with a large tub. The family enjoyed warm baths. There was a washing machine. Nuliaq washed their clothes and soon everything was clean.

Sonny and Nuliaq wanted to cook a large dinner to celebrate their arrival in Fairbanks. They were aware that how close they had come to death while sleeping in the station wagon. Sonny, Nuliaq and Bun were still gaunt and a large dinner to celebrate sounded appetizing.

That night, Sonny and Nuliaq sat on the couch after Bun had bathed and fallen asleep. Nuliaq spoke about how relieved she was that Bun did not suffer any side effects of the carbon monoxide in the station wagon. The toddler had played happily all day with the dog. Bun talked all day while asking questions of Nuliaq about the sights and sounds of their new home in Fairbanks.

Nuliaq continued. She had a menu planned for their dinner. She wanted to go shopping at the store tomorrow. Sonny agreed and the couple happily discussed their plan for the next day of shopping.

The next day was sunny and bright. The icicles on the outside of the little house were dripping as the warm weather continued melting ice and snow during the day. After breakfast, Sonny prepared the station wagon and loaded Bun and the dog on as Nuliaq made a list for shopping. She hummed lightly as she joined Sonny on the station wagon. Sonny carefully steered the car out of the drive and down the street. The wallet in his pants pocket was thick with bills and his heart was full of joy. Sonny felt proud. He wore sunglasses as he drove in the sunlight. Next to him, Nuliaq looked radiant in her sunglasses and golden blond hair. Sonny felt like he was in a magazine picture in his car with his wife in the city.

The streets of Fairbanks were bustling. People emerged from their homes after the weariness of a dark cold winter. Cars sped down the streets in both directions. Sonny drove as Nuliaq pointed out where to turn onto the streets that would lead them to the store. Bun was babbling a silly song as they drove along.

The streets of the main part of the city of Fairbanks were all one way. The streets were crossed by a series of avenues so that city blocks were neatly laid out. The Chena River ran through the heart of Fairbanks, so that the city buildings and streets lay on both sides of the river. Several bridges allowed drivers to cross the city from one side of the river to the other. The layout of the city made it a challenge to find the street where the store was and to navigate the direction so that the car could be parked conveniently in front of the business.

After several drives around the block, Sonny found a parking spot directly in front of the store doors. Feeling a sense of great accomplishment, Sonny smiled at his wife. Nuliaq was staring at the store front. Despite the sunglasses covering Nuliaq's face, Sonny could see her expression of shock and dismay. Sonny immediately glanced at the store front. He could not see what was the cause of his wife's distress. The store doors were normal looking. There was a sheet of white paper on the glass of one door but Sonny could not read it.

Nuliaq began cussing loudly. Sonny jumped in horror. He put a quick hand on Nuliaq's arm and turned a warning look at Bun in the back seat. Bun stopped her singing and frowned. The dog growled softly as he looked out the window but no one was in sight.

Nuliaq apologized for her outburst. She sat a moment. Then, she explained. The paper on the door said, "No drunks, dogs or natives allowed in our store."

Sonny sat back. He felt numb.

Nuliaq hastily suggested that they shop somewhere else. She told Sonny to leave immediately.

Sonny hesitated. The day before, Sonny had talked to the mining company. He had asked where he could buy groceries and other items that his family needed. The man at the mining company office told him about this store and said it was the only one open in Fairbanks to find food and supplies at during this time of the year. Sonny reminded Nuliaq that they could not buy what they needed anywhere else. The couple sat in silence in the car.

Sonny suddenly scoffed. He turned to the back seat and tried to sound lighthearted as he spoke, "You can't go in the store, Spot! You have to wait on the car!"

Bun started giggling. She was too young to understand what was going on and she thought it was funny. She thought her father was silly to think that Spot wanted to go shopping. Sonny continued, "Go ahead, Nuliaq. We will wait for you on the car."

Nuliaq cussed again under her breath before she opened her door. She leaned back in the car and told Sonny she was sorry that this happened. Sonny nodded and waved her on. She walked to the door of the store, pulling her sunglasses off and putting them in her purse.

Sonny sat in the car. He reached into the back seat and tickled Bun. She giggled. Then, Bun returned to playing with Spot while

Sonny sat waiting. He had been looking forward to shopping with his family.

After about 10 minutes, a man came walking down the street. It was a Fairbanks Police officer. The officer scowled as he approached the car where Sonny and Bun waited. He rapped on the window with his night stick. Sonny rolled the window down.

The officer demanded to know why Sonny was in the driver's seat of the car and why he was loitering in front of the store where no natives were allowed. He yelled as he asked if Sonny was drunk.

Sonny replied that he was not drunk.

Sonny felt a sense of alarm and indignation rising in him. He felt fear for Bun. She was frozen in terror in the backseat. Even Spot was sitting in shock.

Sonny got out of the car. He pulled out his wallet and showed the officer his driver's license. The officer eyed the money in the wallet and the driver's license suspiciously. Sonny reached into the glove box for the car registration and handed it to the officer. He explained to the policeman that he had worked at the mining camp all winter and just got paid. Sonny told the officer that he was waiting for his wife who was still shopping in the store. Since the family had been out of town all winter, they needed a lot of goods from the store.

The officer could not find fault with the documents or Sonny's explanation. It was too clear that Sonny was not drunk so the officer had no reason to arrest him. He shoved the license and registration back at Sonny. The policeman stepped back. With the night stick, he pounded the hood of the car so hard it chipped some of the paint. "You have to move this car! You can't park here!" the officer barked and stood with his hands on his hips.

Bun began crying softly. Spot sat beside her on the back seat and growled.

Sonny got back in the car and started it. He gently shushed Bun and tried to reassure her that everything was okay. He pulled the station wagon around the block. Bun began to cry that they had left Mommy in the store. Sonny explained that they just had to move the car. At last, peace was restored.

After a long time, Sonny got out of the car. He walked to the end of the block so he could see the store front. Then, he returned to the car so he would not be loitering.   Sonny repeated this routine until Nuliaq came out of the store. She had a large pile of groceries and supplies packed into boxes. She waved at Sonny to drive down to the doors to load the station wagon. However, the police officer was still standing in front of the store and watching Sonny closely.

Sonny quickly told Bun he was going to talk to Mommy and that he would be out of sight down the street for a bit. He jogged down to the store front. Nuliaq was asking the police officer why Sonny couldn't park in front of the store. The officer pointed to the sign on the door with his stick. Nuliaq pleaded to no avail. The store clerk came out of the door and slammed the last of the boxes of Nuliaq's purchases on the sidewalk. He told her to get everything out of the way. She answered sharply that she and her husband would get their boxes and that they had to carry everything to their car.

Sonny hurried as he carried the boxes back to the station wagon down the block. His brow was wet with perspiration. His sunglasses were foggy. Finally, he picked up the last box, nodded to the store clerk and the police officer, and loaded it in to the station wagon.

The ride home was bittersweet. Nuliaq was happy she had been shopping after a winter at the mining camp. She was delighted with her purchases of food, clothes for every member of the family, dog food for Spot and other supplies. However, a cloud of darkness hung over the family. It was the ugly cloud of racial hatred. Nuliaq began angrily talking about the injustice of the matter, but Sonny shook his head as he nodded towards Bun. He did not want Bun to be frightened further. He did not want his little daughter's joy in the store goods ruined by hate. He wanted to put it behind him.

It was past noon when Sonny drove the station wagon towards their temporary home in the mining company house. After the traffic light, the street crossed the first bridge across the river. Lunch hour traffic was heavy. As the light turned green, Sonny eased the station wagon forward through the light to make his way onto the bridge beyond.

CRASH!

Sonny was knocked out briefly as his forehead slammed into the top of the steering wheel. As he came to, he opened his eyes in confusion. All he could see was red. Blood was flowing down his brow from a cut in his forehead. The blood covered his eyes. He wiped his eyes with his sleeve.

Nuliaq was beside him on the passenger side. Her head had broken the windshield. Her body was slumped halfway across the dashboard.

Sonny tried to turn to look in the back seat to check on Bun. He could not hear his daughter and he was alarmed. Blood blinded his eyes again.

"Hey! It's okay there, mister!" Sonny heard a man's voice and felt hands on his shoulders. "A car hit yours head on. Be still. Help is on the way," the man's voice kept speaking. There were other voices in the background but Sonny couldn't make out the words.

"My daughter…" Sonny mumbled. He tried to point to the back seat. He still could not hear Bun or Spot.

"The drunk driver hit you head on. Everyone is okay in the back seat, Mister. Just stay calm. The ambulance is coming," the man reassured Sonny. He was firmly holding Sonny still in the driver's seat. Sonny blacked out.

Sonny sat on the couch of the mining company house in Fairbanks. He sat thinking and trying to understand what events had led him to this point in time. The day before he had gone shopping. On the way home, a drunk driver had smashed his car into the front of Sonny's car at a traffic light near the bridge in downtown Fairbanks. The drunk driver was traveling extremely fast. Sonny's station wagon was a wreck. Sonny did not care.

Nuliaq lay in bed in the next room. She had a few cuts on her face from breaking through the station wagon windshield at the moment of impact. The doctor at the emergency room said Nuliaq had a concussion and needed to rest for a week.

Sonny was most relieved that Bun was not hurt. She had been pinned by boxes that slid forward from the back of the station wagon. Bun and Spot had been thrown forward by the head on crash into the padded backs of the front car seats. They were both held in place, able to breath despite being stunned, by the boxes.

Sonny gingerly touched his forehead. He had a two inch cut in his forehead from the top of the steering wheel. His entire body felt sore from the jolt of the crash. But, his family was alive. They could easily afford another car.

Sonny rose stiffly from the couch. He checked on Bun. She was playing quietly with the new doll Nuliaq had bought at the store before the car crash. She smiled up at her father broadly. Spot lay nearby. The dog's tail thumped loudly on the wooden floor boards as he looked up at Sonny.

Sonny began unpacking the boxes from the store that kindly strangers had brought from the wrecked station wagon. He put away the groceries and hung the new clothes in the closet or folded them neatly in the dresser drawers. Sonny carefully put all the household supplies on the shelves.

Sonny's stomach growled. He went to the kitchen and studied the cupboard. Several hours later, Sonny laid a meal on the table.

Nuliaq wandered sleepily into the kitchen. She was wondering out loud what smelled so good. She stopped in the doorway when she saw the table and the meal. Nuliaq's blue eyes filled with tears. She hugged Sonny and Bun as they sat waiting at the table. The little family was recovering. From the doorway, Spot's tail thumped on the floor as he wagged it. The dog watched his family eat at the table, wagging his tail in hope.

A week later, Sonny and his family had recovered from the car accident. The police came to the house to get a statement from Sonny and his wife. The drunk driver had been injured and was going to jail as soon as he was released from the hospital. The family of the drunk driver had sent a check to help cover the costs from the car crash.

Sonny and Nuliaq sat on the couch one evening after Bun had gone to bed for the night. It was early April. Most of the snow had melted. Night temperatures still dipped past the freezing point, but spring was eagerly anticipated. The night sky was light now. Fairbanks' location near the Arctic Circle resulted in the arctic white nights. By mid-May the daylight would be bright all night. The stars disappeared from the sky in late April because of the arctic light, and they only returned in early August. With the long days and arctic white nights came a feeling of hope and excitement for the coming summer relief from winter's cold hard darkness.

Sonny discussed with his wife what their plans for the future would be. Sonny said he did not want to stay in Fairbanks. The recent events were difficult and Sonny felt there was a better place to live for his family.

Nuliaq agreed. She had done some research and found out important information. An Alaska Native adult could file with the federal government for a native allotment. If the native person built a home and lived on the allotment for five years, the Bureau of Indian Affairs would grant the native full title to 160 acres of land. The land would be managed in trust by the Bureau. Furthermore, Nuliaq had asked the Bureau of Land Management office in Fairbanks where a native person could find land that was available for claiming a native allotment. There was one place that intrigued Nuliaq. It was almost 300 miles south of Fairbanks. Unlike other areas where allotment land was available, this area had a road that allowed driving access to it. There was a river where salmon could be fished for winter food. There was timber for logs to build a cabin. The soils were good for gardening.

The land that Nuliaq dreamed of was along the Copper River. It was near the little villages of Copper Center, Gulkana and Chitina. There was a larger town called Glennallen. In Glennallen, there were stores, government offices and schools. However, Nuliaq was most taken by one opportunity the area provided. There was a Catholic mission boarding school, called Copper Valley, in the area between Glennallen and the other villages. The mission would provide an education for Bun's future. They could also attend church there.

Sonny agreed that the plan of applying for native allotment land to build their own home on sounded promising. He felt hopeful.

Nuliaq hesitated and then spoke. She wanted to face what she called the elephant in the room. Sonny struggled to imagine an elephant in the room and why Nuliaq would want to talk about it.

Nuliaq recalled the racist sign at the store and the bigoted police officer. She struggled to comprehend the racial problem. It was not easy for her to understand why Sonny was treated like he was. She had never encountered racism before. She began sharing her frustration with Sonny. As his wife, she knew he was smart, hardworking, a good father and husband. Why did he not do more so that other white people could see him in the same way she did? Nuliaq eyed him critically.

Sonny felt a pang of deep pain in his heart. He looked in the blue eyes of his beloved Nuliaq. The woman's eyes were cold again. He felt like the incident at the store made her look at him differently. It was as if she blamed him for the problem and was disappointed in him.

Sonny struggled for words in English. The store incident had been uncomfortable and hurt, especially because Bun had been frightened. Sonny had seen himself as American as any other person in Alaska. He had served his country. He had given his boyhood to be ready to protect the United States.

The State of Alaska was admitted to the Union less than a decade ago. Sonny felt proud of his homeland and proud that Alaska was now a state. He felt like a part of the Alaskan population. It was an exciting time to be an Alaskan. The state's motto was "North to the Future" or the "Last Frontier." A spirit of building and developing the state had covered the land. As a former Territorial Guard, Sonny felt like he had skills and knowledge and hard work to offer building the state. He thought that just as his role in the Territorial Guard was so important that he was signed up as a boy, how much more he could serve his state and country as a full grown man!

Sonny wanted Nuliaq to understand him. He wanted her to accept him for who he was, a Yupik man in the modern age. He had been trained a soldier when he was just a boy instead of living a purely traditional Yupik life subsisting off the land. Although he had told her briefly about his boyhood experience being an Alaska Territorial Guard, he was not sure if she was convinced that he had actually been telling the truth. After all, he had only been a boy when the Alaska Territorial Guard had been formed.

Sonny's wife had proudly told him about her brother in the Army who had been captain of elite forces, the Green Berets, stationed in the Pacific. He had seen how devastated Nuliaq was when her brother was killed in Vietnam shortly before the big earthquake of 1964. Nuliaq's grief was somewhat comforted by the honor the United States had extended to her brother by awarding him a Purple Heart posthumously.

Nuliaq was also proud of her own brief service as a nurse with the Navy at Kodiak. He listened and watched her as she talked. He could tell she was very proud of military service. She knew about the Army in Alaska and also deeply admired Major Marston's leadership. She had nursed some of the Aleut men who had served in the Alaska Territorial Guard. These grown men had seen combat with the Japanese during the height of the war.

Furthermore, Nuliaq admired Alaska Territorial Governor Ernest Gruening for his leadership during the war with the Japanese. She believed that Governor Gruening had done a good job to pave the way for Alaska to become a thriving state within the Union. She pointed out that shortly after Governor Gruening's time in office in 1959, Alaska had become the 49th state in the United States. Nuliaq spoke about the exciting future of Alaska and the fact that William Egan had become the first governor. Alaska was growing and Nuliaq believed big changes were coming.

Nuliaq did not fully comprehend the history of the relationship between the Alaska Natives and the white people who had come to the North to build their future. She could not understand the changes that Alaska had gone through over the years had often been to the detriment of the Native peoples who had lived on the land for tens of thousands of years. Sadly, Native people were struggling for their basic human rights in the face of being governed by non-Native fortune seekers.

In 1915, the Alaska Territorial Legislature imposed legislation that severely restricted Alaska Native voting rights. The law said that Alaska Natives could vote only if they gave up their indigenous culture, customs and traditions. Few Alaska Natives were allowed to vote under this system.

In 1924, the Congress of the United States passed the Indian Citizenship Act. The Act stated that all indigenous people born in the United States were recognized as citizens. The Act allowed for Alaska Natives to vote.

In 1964, the Congress passed the Civil Rights Act. The act prohibited discrimination against any person based on race, color, religion, sex and nationality, but the effect of the act was late in reaching Alaska as signs in the stores or other public establishments still said, "No drunks, dogs, or natives allowed." The practice by white people to mistreat the Natives and their rights had not answered to any authority. Alaska appeared to be too remote, and the lack of care about Alaska Natives kept the system of discrimination, hatred and abuse free of federal oversight. No one came to the frozen North to enforce the Civil Rights Act.

Nuliaq was especially frustrated with Sonny when they were around other white people. She told Sonny afterwards that the white people thought he was drunk or dumb because he did not directly answer their questions. Sonny tried to explain to his wife that when a white person spoke to him, he had to translate the words into Yupik. Next, he had to translate an answer he had made in Yupik back to English. In addition, measured careful thoughtful answers were respected in Yupik culture. Even as he explained, Sonny felt Nuliaq did not believe him or understand. He searched the blue eyes for compassion but only found an icy coldness.

Sonny reflected on the examples of marriages he knew in his life. The Yupik couples, such as his parents, shared the same language and culture. A wealth of relatives of both husband and wife provided support and encouragement, as well as treasuring the children produced by the marriage. The Yupik couple worked hard in a constant subsistence lifestyle year-round, gathering food for their family from the land. When they enjoyed success in raising and feeding their family from the land, the Yupik couple felt a sense of accomplishment that strengthened their love and bonds of marriage.

Sonny had known he would face challenges when he fell in love with a non-Yupik woman. He had also seen marriages between white men and Yupik women around the gold mines of Fortuna Ledge. The women easily adapted and the men worked hard to provide for their wives and children. The mixed marriages found a way to succeed and last. Sonny hoped his marriage would be the same if he worked hard and loved his family. He prayed at the Catholic masses they attended that their union would be blessed.

Sonny smiled at his wife. He agreed to try finding a plot of land to build a Native allotment home on in the Copper River valley. He resolved to be a better husband and father. He would work harder and provide a nice life for his beautiful blue-eyed blonde wife.

THE PLANNING FOR THE FAMILY'S MOVE to the Copper River valley took several months, but the mining company generously allowed Sonny to rent the house until he was ready to leave. The first preparation for the task was to find another vehicle. After weeks of looking, Sonny found a used pickup. It was solid and in excellent condition. He bought some plywood and made a wooden canopy for the back so that the loads were kept dry and safe.

One bright June morning, Sonny was ready to leave Fairbanks. The pickup was packed with all the family's belongings. Spot had a small corner of the back to ride in. Bun had to ride in the cab. She sat on the lap of whichever of her parents was not driving.

When the family stopped for the night, Sonny made a bed in the canopy for them to sleep under warm blankets. Sonny brought a kerosene stove to cook meals on. Two metal five gallon cans carried extra gas and water each. Excited and full of anticipation for new adventures, the family set out driving south 250 miles on the Richardson Highway towards Glennallen.

The journey took two days. It was midafternoon when Sonny pulled into the Copper Valley Catholic boarding school. Nuliaq remarked at the large size of the school buildings.

The school was out of class for the summer. However, the staff was present and busy with preparations for the coming school term. The priests welcomed Sonny and his family. The priests invited the family to dinner in the cafeteria. A room would be prepared for them to sleep in. After a bath and a good night's rest in a comfortable bed, Sonny met with a priest to ask questions and learn more about the area.

The priest described the Copper River valley. He listened carefully as Sonny explained that he was looking for land to apply for a native allotment. The priest liked the idea and suggested that Sonny look for land near Chitina.

Chitina was a tiny ghost town located some 60 miles south of the mission school. The land was drier there and there were large spruce trees for house logs. The land around Glennallen was more boggy than not. The groundwater in Glennallen was full of iron and distasteful. The springs at Chitina were sweet and fresh.

Chitina had been a supply depot along the Copper River Railway, which had been completed in 1911. The trains traveled the railroad from the port of Cordova at the mouth of the Copper River north to the Kennicott mines in the Wrangell Mountains. The railroad was roughly 200 miles long. It ran alongside the Copper River through rugged terrain. Boxcars of copper ore were transported by the railway from the Kennicott mines to be loaded on the ships at the port of Cordova. The trains stopped midway along the route at Chitina to resupply.

In 1938, the mines closed and the trains stopped. The miners, fortune seekers and railroad workers left Alaska. A man bought the town site of Chitina and made it a real ghost town. He painted large ghosts on the fronts of the hotel, stores, garages and other buildings in Chitina. A handful of people remained in the town. The trains had been taken to Cordova. The railroad bed had been plowed up to make a single-lane gravel road from Chitina to the tiny town of McCarthy which lay below the Kennicott mines.

Sonny was familiar with the effects of mines on communities in Alaska. Gold mines had been developed near Fortuna Ledge in 1913. Communities flourished with miners and other people who provided services to the miners, such as traders or post office workers. The transportation needs of the gold mines on the Yukon River were met by barges or steam boats.

Sonny knew that the mining community had an impact on the Native communities that had always lived nearby. He asked the priest about the Native people of Chitina. The priest explained that the indigenous people of the Copper River were Ahtna

Athabaskans. The Ahtna in the Chitina area had been forced to give up their lands and live in an area outside of the town site. The federal government built a school for the Native children separate from the white children in Chitina. The Native village of Chitina thrived during the railroad days. The Ahtna built nice log homes, grew abundant gardens and prospered while working on the railroad. Sadly, when the railroad shut down, the government shut the Native school down too. Ahtna families moved away from Chitina to larger communities for jobs and schools. Only a handful of Native people still lived in Chitina.

The priest told Sonny that the Catholic Church had been given a small one-room house in Chitina. The house was vacant and Sonny was welcome to rent the house for a small amount until he could build his own cabin. Sonny gladly accepted.

The next day, Sonny drove his family to Chitina. He found the painted ghosts on the houses as the priest had said. The town seemed empty, but when Sonny pulled up to the store, he saw it was open. The store clerk welcomed him and listened as he asked directions to the house owned by the Catholic Church. She pointed it out to him. When Nuliaq explained to the clerk about their plans to move to Chitina, the clerk told her the names of several people to talk to show her and Sonny around to choose land.

Soon, Sonny and his wife located the house the priest had rented to them. They moved their possessions, and the next day, they found the people the clerk had mentioned. One was an old prospector, originally from Finland, who had lived in the area through the mining and railroad days. The others were elderly Ahtna. The Ahtna welcomed Sonny. They took him to a place along the Copper River to build his cabin and place his native allotment. They showed him their fish wheel and how the Ahtna harvested salmon from the river.

The Ahtna elders grew close to Sonny. They loved to hear his stories. They admired Sonny's success at hunting and fishing. Sonny quickly learned about the land of the Chitina area.

He quickly staked out the boundaries of his native allotment. He began the design and planning of building his log cabin. At last, the cabin was ready and Sonny moved to his land near Chitina. The first winter passed peacefully as Sonny and his family enjoyed their new home. They made friends with the few people who still lived in Chitina. Spring came early.

Chapter Nineteen

THE AFTERMATH OF WAR
1967

LIFE IN CHITINA LOOKED PROMISING FOR Sonny, Nuliaq and Bun.

Sonny's new log cabin stood on top of a high bluff overlooking the Copper River. Towering over the cabin to the west was a mountain, the Ahtna elders called Kylee. To the north of the cabin was the spectacular beauty of the Wrangell St. Elias mountain range. The land that Sonny's native allotment stood on was abundant with life and natural resources. The soil was rich. Sonny cleared the thick grass near the cabin for a garden plot. The plot faced the warmth and brightness of the sun shining from the south. He planted potatoes, carrots, turnips and carrots.

The new fish wheel was anchored on the river bank below the bluff. It was ready to be eased into the river when the salmon began running past on their way upstream. Sonny built drying racks to hang the fish and prepare them for the winter.

There were plenty of moose, rabbits and game birds. There

were abundant patches of raspberries and currants. The water in the nearby creeks was sweet and pure. There were thick stands of spruce that were good for firewood or building logs. The Ahtna elders told Sonny that trapping was great around his cabin. There were wolves, wolverine and lynx to be caught.

Sonny surveyed his cabin and land. Bun was playing with Spot. Nuliaq was inside the cabin baking bread. He could hear her humming as she kneaded the dough. He decided everything was in good order. All that was needed was a way to earn money to buy the supplies he could not provide from the land. It was time to look for work.

Sonny discussed the idea of working with Nuliaq. She agreed that he needed to go into town to find out if there were any opportunities for earning wages there. Her brow knotted as she frowned. It would be difficult if he had to go to the nearby towns to find work. However, she was determined to make sure their new life worked.

Sonny drove into town. It was quiet. He stopped at the store and went inside. The store clerk greeted him and listened as he asked about work. She nodded and told him to accompany her to her sister's house. Sonny followed the clerk as they walked to a house down the street.

The store clerk entered and emerged a moment later to bring Sonny inside. She introduced Sonny to her brother-in-law. The brother-in-law was a guide and a bush pilot. The pilot wanted to hire Sonny to drive big construction equipment on the gravel road on the railroad bed from Chitina to McCarthy. The job would start immediately in the spring and last until the winter snow closed down the work. Sonny was hesitant to leave his wife and daughter alone at the cabin. A lot of work around the home still needed to be done before winter. The pilot told him to talk the matter over with his wife and let him know the next day.

Sonny returned to his cabin. He told Nuliaq about the pilot and the job that he was offered. Sonny spoke to her about his reluctance to take the job because he would be gone all summer.

Nuliaq frowned. She had not liked the store clerk since the two met. After she realized he would be staying in Chitina, Nuliaq shared with Sonny that she did not trust the store clerk or her sister. Now, after thinking about the situation, Nuliaq told Sonny that they needed the money. She would work hard to take care of the garden, put up the salmon and berries for the winter. He would work for the pilot until autumn. It was not ideal but it was the choice they needed to take.

Sonny felt a pit of dread in his stomach that evening. He watched Bun playing in the yard. He would miss his daughter's laughter and dimpled smile. Nuliaq joined him as he stood watching Bun. She hugged Sonny and whispered. She was happy. She thanked her husband for the new home and the rich property and the new life that looked so full of promise. Sonny hugged her back. A tiny spark of hope kindled inside of him.

Early the next morning, Nuliaq drove Sonny into town. She left him at the pilot's house. She and Bun said goodbye. Spot wagged his tail. Sonny knocked on the door and went inside. The pilot was waiting. He planned on leaving immediately. Sonny reluctantly left with the pilot to work for the summer season.

When the snow fell in September, Sonny finally returned home. The pilot flew him from McCarthy to Chitina late in the day. Sonny waited at the store for his wife to pick him up. He was tired. The pilot told him to stay at his house for the night since it was late. The next day, the pilot would drive Sonny to his cabin and family.

Sonny wearily agreed to spend one more night away from his family. The pilot took him to his home. After eating dinner, the pilot pulled out a bottle of whiskey. Sonny told him that he did not want to drink. He just wanted to rest and go home, but the pilot insisted that Sonny join him. The air became tense as the pilot looked as if he was becoming dangerously angry at Sonny. Sonny accepted a drink.

Sonny woke the next morning with a hangover. He tried to remember when he got into bed the night before but his head hurt and his mind was foggy. The pilot was in a surly mood as he drove Sonny home. He thrust an envelope at Sonny when they arrived, saying it was Sonny's pay for the summer. The pilot drove off in a cloud of dust.

Nuliaq met Sonny at the door with open arms. Suddenly, she stepped back frowning. "Have you been drinking?!" she asked in a mixture of anger and surprise. Sonny explained what had happened the night before and how the pilot had insisted that he drink with him. He handed Nuliaq the envelope and went outside to find Bun.

Sonny felt a pang in his heart when he found Bun in the garden with Spot. His daughter was much taller. She looked shyly at him. She hesitated to go to him. Spot growled a little and whined. Sonny felt he had been away too long. Bun slowly warmed up and took his hand to show him the plants she was growing in the garden. Sonny told her how proud he was of her. She smiled up at him as they walked back to the cabin.

When Bun and Sonny reached the cabin, Nuliaq was waiting at the door. She told Bun to go back to the garden to finish weeding it. She pulled Sonny inside and thrust the envelope at him. For the first time in their marriage, Nuliaq began screaming at Sonny.

The envelope held an IOU for several hundred dollars to the pilot. The note said that Sonny had used up his paycheck for the summer's work on a bet and lost. Sonny kept drinking whiskey and insisted on an IOU to repay for the alcohol. Sonny was stunned. He stared at the note dumbly.

The IOU was the beginning of the end for Sonny and his marriage to Nuliaq. No matter how often he told Nuliaq that the pilot was lying, she did not believe him. Life at the cabin was tense and Sonny felt unwelcome.

Nuliaq was angry. She wrote to her family and borrowed money to make it through the winter. She quit speaking to Sonny.

Bun began to huddle in the corner of the cabin. She looked at her parents with large frightened eyes. Spot lay at her feet as if protecting her.

Sonny tried to talk to the pilot. The store clerk told him that her sister and the pilot were out of town for most of the winter. Sonny tried to explain what had happened and ask the store clerk to reimburse him the wages he earned during the summer.

The store clerk listened until Sonny asked to have his wages reimbursed. Her face grew red and her eyes became cold. She told him that he foolishly drank away his wages and she could not help him. Sonny left the store. Overhead, the gray skies of September seemed dark and dismal.

With no other option, Sonny left Chitina to look for work to pay back the IOU and support his family through the winter. He packed a green Army surplus duffle bag with his clothes. The look of fear, confusion and loss on Bun's face as he left the cabin was seared into his mind. He tried to concentrate on moving forward towards a job. Working to pay his unjust debt and support his family was his path back to Bun.

The journey began with his walking out of the town along the dirt road. He planned to hitch a ride as far as the nearest town and look for construction work. After walking a couple of miles, Sonny began to wonder if how far he was going to have to walk. The nearest town was over 50 miles away. Finally, he could hear the rumble of a truck approaching. It was a state road construction worker. Sonny recognized the driver as an Ahtna man from the area. The truck stopped as the worker asked Sonny where he was going. When Sonny explained, the worker agreed to drive him to the nearest town. Along the way, the worker chatted with Sonny. The worker listened as Sonny shared his plight with the pilot and the stolen wages. He told Sonny that most native people avoided the pilot because of the same problem of being given alcohol and a debt.

Sonny learned that it was going to be hard to find a job in construction anywhere nearby. The worker told Sonny that the best place to find a job was near Anchorage. The worker dropped Sonny off at gas station where travelers stopped on their way to the city. Hitchhikers found success in catching a ride to Anchorage by waiting there. The worker bought Sonny a coffee and sandwich and wished him luck in finding work.

After several hours of waiting at the gas station, Sonny found a ride to Anchorage. To his surprise a man approached him as he sat waiting. Sonny looked up. The man was a fellow Eskimo. The man smiled and asked Sonny if he needed a ride. Sonny nodded. The man replied that he was going to Anchorage and could give him a ride. Sonny gratefully accepted.

The man introduced himself as Buddy. He steered his truck out of the town towards Anchorage. Buddy turned to Sonny and said that he was going to pick his wife up from their cabin that was a few miles along the way.

Buddy's wife, Mona, was Ahtna. She warmly greeted Sonny as he moved to the back seat next to his duffle bag. The drive to Anchorage was short. Sonny found the conversation with the native couple fascinating.

Buddy had also been in the Alaska Territorial Guard as a young man. He was Inupiaq from a village near Nome. Buddy was among 65 men chosen by Colonel Castner for a special effort in the war against Japan. Colonel Castner had been tasked with organizing a Special Forces platoon, the First Alaskan Combat Intelligence Platoon. The men were minimally outfitted and equipped. They had to survive in the harsh conditions of the land by using all the survival skills they had gained by living in remote Alaska. The group of men were Aleut, Inupiaq, Athabaskan as well as non-native prospectors and seasoned sourdoughs who trapped and hunted off the land.

This special unit of hearty men were the Alaskan Scouts. Their mission was to do whatever they needed to do to get the job done. The men answered the call and earned their name, "Castner's Cutthroats."

The Alaskan Scouts lived off the land as they were assigned reconnaissance work on the Aleutian Islands. The islands of Attu and Kiska had been invaded by the Japanese, and the Army had sent the Alaskan Scouts to find a way to attack the Japanese and drive them out of Alaska.

The Army had been struggling to develop a plan to attack the islands and defeat the Japanese, so the Scouts went to the nearby islands and studied the situation. They warned the Army that the use of conventional military vehicles was not possible on the island terrain.

37 Alaskan Scouts were taken by the U.S. Navy submarines to Adak Island. When the Scouts landed, they reconnoitered the island for Japanese. No enemies were found. The Scouts were then tasked with damming the lagoon and building an airstrip. The airstrip allowed the Army to use the forward air base for supply planes to avoid further losses due to crashes in unfavorable weather conditions.

The Scouts supported Army troops stationed on the islands through the winter by building shelters and harvesting food, and they provided vital intelligence to the Army about the Japanese presence on the islands.

Finally, in mid-May, 1933, the Army attacked the Japanese strongholds on Attu. In Operation Landcrab, Canadian pilots assisted with reconnaissance and bombing. An amphibious assault was coordinated by the U. S. Navy to land troops on the beaches. The weather conditions were brutally cold and stormy.

Japanese warships attempted to rally in an effort to reinforce their soldiers on Attu. However, the U.S. Navy thwarted the plan and the Japanese soldiers on Attu were abandoned.

After weeks of heavy mortar rounds and naval bombardment, the Japanese became desperate and attacked the trenches of the American soldiers on the island. The Japanese soldiers swarmed down the slopes in an effort to overwhelm the Army. They broke through a section of the Army line of defense. Hand-to-hand combat broke out. Men fought toe to toe with bayonet, knifes and pistols for their lives. It was a violent battle. Most of the Japanese died in the brutal combat. The Scouts and the Army soldiers were fighting for the protection of their homeland. The thought of the safety of their families back home gave the men courage and success on the battlefield.

The Battle of Attu was hard fought and won at a terrible cost. The death toll for the Japanese Imperial Army was over two thousand and three hundred men. Japanese Imperial Army Colonel Yamasaki died in the fighting. 27 of his men were taken as prisoners of war. Over 1,000 American soldiers were injured. 549 brave soldiers of the 7th Infantry gave their lives for the fight to protect U.S. soil.

The Army continued to clear Japanese soldiers in small hideouts from the islands through September, 1943. Earlier in late July, 1943, the Japanese had covertly removed their forces from Kiska Island in the Aleutian Chain. The Japanese military occupation on American soil had ended.

As Buddy drove, he told Sonny that he could not relate details of his service as an Alaskan Scout. The Scouts were ordered to keep their service classified. Sonny told Buddy that he had heard of the Battle of Attu from his Alutiiq friend on Kodiak. Buddy admired Sonny for serving in the Territorial Guard as a boy. Sonny countered that he admired the work that the Alaskan Scouts had done in their service.

Sonny grew somber after reaching Anchorage. There was no recognition for the men and women who served in the Territorial Guard. The country he served to protect did not value his contribution. However, Sonny was resolved to continue his efforts in upholding the values he learned as a Yupik in the Alaska Territorial Guard. He struggled to find work because he couldn't read, but he found work in Anchorage as a seasonal plow driver. He worked hard that first winter and made sure he sent money home to Nuliaq. He kept only enough money from his pay to rent a rough room in a lodging. He lay in bed every night, unable to sleep because of the noisy neighbors who were drunk every day.

Sonny wondered how Bun was faring. The pain of missing Bun was almost too much to bear. On weekends, Sonny began to spend the days in the bar. He tried to drown the pain he felt when he thought of his daughter.

In the spring, a letter came from Nuliaq. Sonny had to get a coworker to read it to him. Nuliaq thanked Sonny for the money but it wasn't enough to cover all of their needs. Despite being without enough money, she wrote that she and Bun were happy. She begged him not to come back to the cabin or Chitina. She did not want Sonny to return to cause trouble with the pilot. The pilot proved to be a man who should be avoided, which she managed to do. Furthermore, she refused to raise Bun around anyone who drank. Nuliaq had heard rumors that Sonny was drinking on weekends.

The years began to pass. Sonny began to wander around Alaska, always looking for work that he could be hired for without being able to read or write. He returned to Kodiak in the hopes that he could find work as a commercial fisherman. He found the bear guide he had worked for before the earthquake. The guide hired him again as back up gun for bear hunts and as a commercial fishing deckhand. Sonny told him to give his pay to Nuliaq for Bun. When the guide was not hunting or fishing, Sonny waited the time between his work seasons in the bar. He found that whiskey helped him forget Nuliaq and Bun.

One year, Sonny asked the guide to write to Nuliaq. He wanted to see Bun. When the guide received Nuliaq's reply, he read the letter which said that Bun should not to see Sonny. She was happy without her father. Sonny grew quiet and threw himself into work. When the work ended, Sonny threw himself into whiskey bottles.

However, Sonny maintained his core Yupik values. Whatever company he was in, he told stories. Soon, his listeners would be laughing. Sonny tried hard to put everything in a good light.

Years passed.

Sonny never returned home to Tuckchuck. The village had become almost deserted as Yupik people moved away for schools or work. Aata and Aana died. Nayagaq was happily married and had four children of her own. She continued to live in nearby villages along the Yukon River where her children could attend school. Sonny kept in touch with her through various relatives he crossed paths with while in Anchorage. Nayagaq sent word that Kuukuq was living in Bethel. She worried about the kind of life he was living and that he was drinking too much. She invited Sonny to come home and stay with her family. She missed her big brother.

Sonny began to stay in Kodiak full time. He did not like Anchorage. Throughout the late 1960s and mid-1970s, Anchorage grew in population and changed. More native people were living on the streets, homeless and abusing alcohol. Crowds of people seeking work on the Trans Alaska Pipeline moved to Alaska from Texas and Oklahoma. More people arrived seeking to make their fortunes off of the pipeline workers through prostitution, drug dealing or illegal gambling.

Television, telephones and movies were now available throughout the cities of Alaska. Sonny watched the changes take over the state. He felt lost. Or he felt like he had lost everything. The worst part of the loss Sonny felt was the loss of hope in a good life away from his Yupik childhood. In his dreams, memories of his happy childhood in Tuckchuck filled his mind. The love of Aata and Aana and stable simple home that Aata provided made him feel safe. The love of the elders of Tuckchuck and the beauty of the Yupik language would visit him in the night. The beauty of the land, such as the northern lights dancing as his dog team flew down a snowy trail, brought a smile Sonny's face as he slumbered.

When he awakened, Sonny recalled the simplicity of life he enjoyed before he joined the Territorial Guard and the war was not a threat looming over his coming of age. One day, Sonny was watching television as the news showed footage of Vietnam after

Agent Orange was sprayed on the jungles of the battlefield. He watched the destruction of the land as the newscaster spoke the words 'the aftermath of war.'

Suddenly, everything made sense to Sonny. It was the aftermath of war. His life was the aftermath of war. Sonny felt it in his spirit, his mind and his body. The boy warrior had grown old.

SONNY TRAVELED TO ANCHORAGE TO SEE the doctor. His body was wearing out from years of hard labor. His right knee was so damaged by arthritis he could only limp. He walked through the hospital building to his doctor's appointment.

There sat Nuliaq.

Sonny sat next to his wife and asked her how she was doing. Nuliaq said she needed surgery but she would be fine. She looked at Sonny with her blue eyes.

Sonny asked if he could visit Bun. Nuliaq shook her head. Bun was gone from home. She was attending high school at a Catholic mission boarding school. Nuliaq told Sonny that their daughter was smart and getting a good education. Bun had a bright future ahead of her and Nuliaq wanted her to go to college right after high school.

Nuliaq told Sonny that the native allotment would go to Bun. She had already drawn up the papers for Bun to get the land after either of her parents died.

Nuliaq had left the cabin in Chitina. After her surgery, Nuliaq was moving and hoped to go back to work as a nurse. She explained she was moving back to the state where she had grown up on the East Coast of the country. She said Bun would join her there when their daughter went on summer break from boarding school. She looked at Sonny again. She told him that he had never sent enough money for Bun. If he had sent more money, life would have been easier for their daughter.

Sonny frowned. He told Nuliaq that he had arranged for the

guide to send almost all of his money every paycheck. The paychecks for the commercial fishing seasons were quite big.

Nuliaq shook her head. Her blue eyes looked angry. She did not believe him.

Sonny realized that the guide had kept most of the money he had given him to send to Nuliaq. He told Nuliaq that the guide had taken the money.

Nuliaq and Sonny sat in the doctor's waiting room in silence.

After a long time, the nurse came to call Nuliaq into the exam room. Nuliaq turned to Sonny. Sonny saw tears well up his wife's beautiful blue eyes as she wished him well. Sonny wished her the same. It was the last time Sonny saw his beloved wife.

As Sonny waited his turn to see the doctor, he thought of the ancient Yupik legend of how the crane got its blue eyes. As a boy, he thought that the crane was innovative and intelligent for substituting blue berries for his stolen eyes. As a young man, he had looked into his woman's blue eyes and fell in love as if falling in a pool of blue water.

Now, he sighed. His wife's eyes had become less welcoming. Sonny realized that he had never fully understood the legend of how the crane got its blue eyes and its lesson. He had looked at the blue beauty of Nuliaq's eyes. However, Nuliaq had looked at the world and saw what she wanted to see in a blue world of her own. First, she had wanted to live in Kodiak and he had moved there to please her. Then, after the destruction of the 1964 earthquake, she had wanted to live in remote Interior Alaska at a gold mining camp with only the wild land around her. Then, she had wanted to live in Chitina on Sonny's native allotment. She looked at Sonny differently because of the treachery of the pilot. However, Nuliaq had stayed in the cabin Sonny built and kept his land to pass on to their daughter Bun.

Nuliaq's blue eyes had changed from warm blue pools to cold ice. Sonny sighed again. He felt no animosity towards Nuliaq. How could he? He saw the world through Yupik eyes. Nuliaq saw the world differently. A peaceful feeling overcame Sonny as he let Nuliaq go in his heart.

When Sonny's turn came, the doctor had bad news. Sonny was dying. His heart was giving out. The years of hard physical labor combined with the lungs damaged by tuberculosis were too much for Sonny's heart. The doctor told him that there was not much that he could do. He advised Sonny to get his affairs in order.

Sonny left the doctor's office deep in thought. He felt a wave of gratitude wash over him as he walked from the hospital back to the room he was renting. Aana's words whispered in his ear as he walked, "Agayutem auluksugatem." *God cares about you!* Sonny remembered his mother's arms around him as a young boy and her words whispered in his ear giving him great comfort and calm.

Ellam Yua was the Yupik word for God. Aana and Aata told Sonny that the Yupik people knew of God and Jesus Christ as taught by the Roman Catholic missionaries from ages before. The knowledge of the Catholic faith's monotheistic God was easily accepted, embraced and followed by the Yupik people because of the familiarity of their ancient belief in Agayun and Ellam Yua, the one God and Creator. The gratitude, the rules for a good life and the dedication to helping one another were Yupik values that translated easily to Catholicism.

Sonny knew his path forward and the knowledge gave him solace.

Along the walk home to his rental, Sonny passed the white Catholic cathedral in downtown Anchorage. The bells of the cathedral were ringing. Sonny went inside the large wooden doors.

"Bless me, Father, for I have sinned," Sonny knelt in the confessional at the far corner of the cathedral. "It has been over twenty five years since my last confession."

Sonny told the priest of his failure of his marriage to Nuliaq and his abandonment of Bun. He confessed his bitterness of being a helpless victim of racial hatred all the years of his adulthood even though he had served his nation as a Territorial Guard.

Sonny confessed the pain of the wrongs he had experienced from the stealing of his hard earned money by the pilot in Chitina and the guide in Kodiak. As he confessed, Sonny felt the heaviness and pain of his heart lifted with each word. He added that he failed as a son to his parents by leaving his village and abandoning them in their old age. He had not been present for Aata's or Aana's death or funeral.

The priest spoke kindly when Sonny finished. He told Sonny that he was forgiven everything and that God loved him deeply. God also loved Nuliaq and Bun and would provide for them. With a deep sense of having made it right with God, Sonny left the church.

Sonny booked and paid for a flight from Anchorage to Bethel and on to Pilot Station where his sister now lived. He had called the bear hunting guide to tell him that he could not return to Kodiak to work any longer. He gathered his few belongings and headed home to the Yukon River.

When Sonny arrived in Tuutalgaq, or Pilot Station, he found Nayagaq. He did not tell Nayagaq that he was dying, but he wondered if she knew death was the reason he had returned home after decades of absence. She was overcome with emotion as she greeted Sonny. She and her husband were going back to fish camp for the rest of the silver salmon and chum salmon season. Sonny would come with them.

Sonny felt a great sense of joy as he joined his sister and her family at the fish camp. His brother-in-law was a quiet hard working Yupik man who reminded Sonny of Aata. Nayagaq's oldest son was the same age as Sonny was when Muktuk Marston had signed him up for the Territorial Guard. Sonny's nephew was immediately devoted to his uncle. He stayed by Sonny's side all day, asking him questions and listening to his stories.

The richness and depth of speaking the Yupik language returned to Sonny. Yupik was the language of fish camp. The difficulty of having to translate English into Yupik and a Yupik answer into English disappeared. Sonny felt relieved as his thoughts came clearly and easily. He wondered how death would find him. He wondered if he had been away from his Yupik land too long to find his way to his eternal home.

Chapter Twenty

MOTHER'S ARMS
1978

SONNY DREW BACK TO THE PRESENT at the fish camp. In his hand, the coffee cup was half full and cold. The sun was now up. Its bright rays were flooding the yard with warmth. Inside the tent, Nayagaq was stirring. Sonny had reminisced long enough. His life on this earth was ending. He felt at peace. People had taken his money, mistreated him over his race and his marriage failed. However, he had been a man of courage. He had been a tan'gurraq, a boy warrior because he could not simply be a growing boy. The importance of his role in helping to protect Alaska from the invading Japanese during World War II demanded Sonny grow up fast. He had to be an anguyak, the same warrior as all the grown men of his village. Sonny had done the best he could every step of his life. It had not been easy, but Sonny had met the challenges with the only way he knew how… as a Yupik man.

Sonny's nephew emerged from the tent. He looked sleepy until he spied Sonny on the bench. The boy eagerly joined Sonny, asking him how long he had been awake and sitting outside on the bench.

Sonny tousled the boy's hair and teased him about being a sleepy head. He explained that he himself had risen early. The boy asked why, wondering if Sonny had a bad dream. Sonny shook his head. He explained to his nephew that he had had some thinking to do. The boy nodded.

Sonny studied his nephew in the morning sun. Inside the tent, the sounds of Nayagaq's younger children's voices rose as they dressed. The young voices were full of eagerness to start the new day.

Sonny turned to his nephew. His nephew loved Sonny's stories. Sonny found he deeply enjoyed telling stories to his nephew and making the boy laugh. Sonny and the boy spent many hours at the fish camp on the bench, talking and laughing. Sometimes, Nayagaq would join in. Other times, she spoke from the tent as if she had been listening to every word.

Sonny began his morning story. It was the story about the morning after he shot the bear and his mother wakened him to go with his family to Fortuna Ledge. As Sonny recalled that morning to his nephew, it seemed so long ago that it was like a dream he had dreamed.

Sonny gazed across the yard as he spoke. He turned the account of his memory into a humorous lesson. He spoke of how tired he had been that morning long ago and how he wanted to sleep. The words in Yupik were filled with humor. His nephew began laughing at the picture the words shaped in his mind of his sleepy uncle. Sonny laughed too. He added, "All I wanted to do was roll over and go back to sleep!" Sonny leaned to the side as if he were going back to sleep.

As Sonny leaned over, the sunlight hit his face. He shut his eyes against the brilliance. "Sonny." A familiar voice whispered in Sonny's ear.

As Sonny leaned, he felt himself slip. He was shrinking. He slid off the bench. Sonny was small again. He felt arms pick him up.

"Aana?!" Sonny opened his eyes.

There was Aana. Aata was at her shoulder, looking at Sonny and smiling. Aata's and Aana's faces were glowing with love.

"You are home!" Aana kissed Sonny's face. He sank into her embrace. "Come!" Aana continued, "Your grandparents are waiting for us! All of your relatives are here!"

As Aana rose, Sonny looked down. Below, he could see the bench. His nephew was shaking an old shrunken form of a man slumped on his side on the bench. The tent flap opened. Nayagaq emerged. She was wailing but the sound of her cry was fading as Aata and Aana, with Sonny in her arms, ascended into the sky where all was bright and warm.

Chapter Twenty-One

THE SECRET PURPOSE
2007

BUN STARED AT THE ENVELOPE. THE return address was that of the United States Army. Her hand shook as she opened the seal, and slowly, she pulled out the brown envelope's contents. It was a green plastic folder. She felt numb as she opened the folder and read the words as tears welled up in her eyes. It was Sonny's honorable discharge from the United States Army for his service in the Alaska Territorial Guard.

65 years after Sonny had signed the Territorial Guard form with his father in the presence of Major Muktuk Marston, the Army discharged him.

The irony was not lost on Bun. She murmured, "Aata, you are free. Quyana! Thank you for your service."

Bun wiped her tears and paused a moment in thought. It seemed so long ago when her father had walked out of the cozy cabin he had built for her and her mother. She did not understand what was going on. She had broken into tears and could not be consoled. After a time, Nuliaq gave up trying to console Bun and warned her to stop crying.

Bun had swallowed her tears. She had swallowed the pain of knowing she would never see her father again.

Through the years, Bun had learned about life. She had learned that it was taboo to speak about her father. Nuliaq would become angry. Her mother could not accept her father's failures and blamed his poor character on alcoholism. Bun had put her thoughts and memories of her father aside and thrown herself into her studies. She excelled in her schoolwork.

Leaving the cabin her father had built on his native allotment near Chitina to go almost a thousand miles away to attend Catholic Mission boarding school had been difficult. Bun had turned to her studies again. She worked part-time during high school. When it came time to attend college, she was easily accepted.

College, a career and marriage. Bun moved through life.

Nuliaq, Bun's mother, returned to work as a nurse. She moved from Alaska to rejoin her family on the East Coast, and Bun visited her mother several times. The white relatives met Bun with a cool attitude. Bun gave them the benefit of the doubt that they were not racist against her for being half Yupik. She did not know how to relate comfortably to her mother's relatives. She was sure they did not know how to relate to Bun in return. The distance between the East Coast cultures and the western Alaskan Yupik was too immense.

When Sonny died, she flew to the Yupik village to bury him. Her aunt greeted Bun at the tiny village airport.

Bun was taken to her aunt's house where Sonny's humble coffin lay in the center of the cabin. Many Yupik relatives came to pay respect. She was told by her Yupik relatives how the last days of her father's life passed. As she listened to Sonny's final days as he returned to fish camp with his sister, emotion swelled up in Bun. She began to weep at the thought of her father finally returning home to die among his Yupik family. Sonny died at the fish camp along the Yukon River that he loved so much as a child.

Nayagaq rushed to Bun's side and held her close. "Don't cry!" Nayagaq begged Bun. "Sonny is looking at you! He does not want to see you sad and crying!" Bun swallowed her tears and buried deep in her heart her sorrow for her father.

The Yupik people buried Sonny on a beautiful bluff overlooking the mighty Yukon River. Sonny's grave lay next to his mother's. Bun felt nothing but emptiness as she left the next day.

Decades passed.

One day, Bun saw a new item on the internet news that sparked a vague memory. The U.S. Army was discharging all the members of the Alaska Territorial Guard from service. Bun recalled that her mother had mentioned Sonny had been a Guard member when he was a boy. Bun had not spoken to Nuliaq in almost two years. She picked up the phone and dialed her mother's number.

When Nuliaq answered, she sounded surprised. "I was just about to call you this week! I wanted to tell you myself instead of you hearing it from someone else. I received my court papers yesterday. My name change was granted and my maiden name is restored."

Bun was silent. Nuliaq continued, "I still love you, Bun. I just don't want to be known by your father's name. He is gone."

Bun explained her reason for calling. She asked if her mother wanted to file for the discharge papers. There was a possibility that Nuliaq could receive benefits as a military spouse.

Nuliaq was emphatic. She refused to take part in any matters involving Sonny and told Bun to handle everything concerning her father.

Their conversation ended.

Bun called her aunt Nayagaq, who confirmed that Sonny had served in the Guard. Nayagaq urged Bun to submit papers to Army for honorable discharge. She hoped Bun could tell the Army to put a headstone on Sonny's unmarked grave. Bun agreed.

She filed the forms for honorable discharge with the Army using the dates of her father's service in the Alaska Territorial Guard provided by her aunt. She had almost forgotten about the matter when a brown envelope from the Army arrived in the mail.

Bun stared at the discharge papers. She thought of her father, and her favorite memory came to her mind. When Bun was three years old, her mother had read her favorite book to her every night before bed. It was the story of Bambi.

One winter evening, Bun felt bored and wanted to hear the book read to her. Her mother was cooking at the wood stove. She wiped the perspiration from her forehead with impatience as she told Bun that she was too busy cooking to stop and read her book. Bun insisted. Her mother told Bun to ask her father to read the book.

Bun hesitated. Sonny had never read a book to her. She was too young to understand that he could not read. Now, as an adult she understood that Sonny had served in the Guard instead of learning to do so.

Sonny invited Bun onto his lap and took the book in his hands. He slowly turned the pages. As he and Bun looked through the pictures of Bambi, Sonny told a new story about the little deer. At first, Bun wanted to protest that the story that Sonny was telling was not the one her mother had read to her a hundred times before, but the story that Sonny unfolded fascinated Bun. It was new and exciting. Bun was enthralled. She reluctantly hopped down from her father's lap when her mother finished cooking and it was time to eat.

Bun could not put the experience into words, but she witnessed the truth that both her parents could relate a great story in different ways. Although Bun learned to love reading and books from her mother, she knew Sonny had knowledge of storytelling in a different but rich and exciting way. From then on, Bun loved to listen to Sonny's stories. He did not need a book to tell a great story.

When Sonny left the family to find work, Bun threw herself into books. She wondered if she was looking for her father and his story somewhere in all the hundreds of books she had read.

As Bun held the honorable discharge document from the Army with Sonny's name on it, she suddenly smiled. She had never found her father in any of the books she read, but now, Bun found her father in the idea of writing a book. She resolved to carry on the tradition of storytelling her parents had raised her with. She would write about her father and his brave service as a boy in the Alaska Territorial Guard during World War II so others could read it.

Bun's resolve to write her father's story as a book welled inside her. She had grown up with the shaming stigma of an absent father. She had heard relatives on her mother's side speak of Sonny as a failed father. This failure did not reconcile with what her Yupik relatives said about Sonny in honest praise when she chanced to meet them in passing. Bun drew a deep breath as understanding grew within her. Her father had loved her. He might have failed as a father in the conventional way, but he had not failed as a man. In fact, he had been forced to become a man early. He had served as a Guard member when his country asked him to help fight the war. He had used his Guard training to overcome challenges for the rest of his life.

Bun smile grew as she chuckled. She recalled something she had read somewhere: "A daughter's smile is the secret purpose of every father." At the time Bun read the quote, she had wondered the meaning in vain. Now, she understood. In a strange way, the Army discharge paper she held brought healing from the decades of painful loss from her father's absence.

Honorable discharge.

Her father had been an honorable man.

Honor at last.

GROWING UP ON THE BANKS OF the Copper River, Aurora Hardy read voraciously. Without electricity or modern conveniences, while homeschooling, Aurora entertained herself by reading. Aurora also wrote, keeping a journal, making a "newspaper" and recording the beauty of the land in poetry. She was published several times in Howard Rock's Alaska Native newspaper, *The Tundra Times*. In 1986, Aurora was the first Native woman to graduate from the University of Montana School of Forestry. Her work demanded technical and scientific report writing, but Aurora always dreamed of writing her own stories. In 2007, she published *Terror at Black Rapids*, about a terrorist attack on the Alaska Pipeline. As she worked, raised children, and became a grandparent, Aurora wrote stories and poems. In 2025, *The Ghost of the Kenai* was published by Epicenter Press. Aurora continues to enjoy writing, fishing for salmon, and walking near her home in South Central Alaska. Aurora is dedicated to inspire reading to young Alaskans.